THE GREEK DOCTOR'S PROPOSAL

BY
MOLLY EVANS

First published in Great Britain 2009
Harlequin Mills & Boon Limited,
Eton House, 18-24 Paradise Road, Richmond, Surrey TW9 1SR

ISBN: 978 0 263 86857 9

Set in Times Roman 10½ on 12¾ pt
03-0709-42724

Printed and bound in Spain
by Litografia Rosés, S.A., Barcelona

THE GREEK DOCTOR'S PROPOSAL

CHAPTER ONE

Albuquerque, NM, USA

SO MANY times Jeannine Carlyle had walked into a hospital as a nurse. Then for a time she had been a patient. This time as she entered the pediatric ICU of a large teaching hospital, she was going to put the last six months behind her and put her life back together. So much about her had been changed, but being a nurse and wanting to help people had not. Lying flat on her back after a life-threatening miscarriage and months of rehab hadn't changed that, but had only made her conviction stronger.

After entering the ICU, she approached the nurse manager. "Hi, Arlene."

"Jeannine, glad to see you here bright and early." Arlene glanced over Jeannine, assessing her attire. "You found the right color scrubs, I see."

"Sure did," Jeannine said, and looked down at her royal blue outfit. "Slightly different than the last place I worked, but I needed new scrubs anyway." The weight loss she had suffered recently had made her previous scrubs entirely too large. Though spring had blossomed and the weather was warming, she wore a longsleeved T-shirt beneath the scrubs to cover the healing marks on her arms. Trying not to be overly conscious of them, she tried to ignore them, hoping that if she didn't draw attention to them no one else would notice her disfigurement. There were no scars on her face, but she felt every one of them as if they were all visible. She knew they would heal, but the inside of her that hurt the most might never recover.

"Well, glad to have you on board." Arlene began to walk down the hall further into the PICU. "We'll be having grand rounds soon. Our medical director, Dr. Kyriakides, will be presenting a very interesting case we had a few months back. I can introduce you to some of the staff first."

"Sounds great." A good way to get to know some of the staff without having to jump in with both feet on her first day on the job. What a relief.

Arlene hesitated outside a large conference-room door. "Are you sure you're ready for this? Coming back to work, I mean?"

Jeannine felt her stomach slide. "Are you having reservations about me being here?"

"No, I'm not. Your résumé and references more than proved you're a very capable nurse. It's just that the pediatric ICU can be a very emotionally difficult place to work at times." Arlene's compassionate gaze searched Jeannine's face.

"Yes, I know," Jeannine said, and hoped the redness she felt in her face wasn't too visible. "But I have to start somewhere sometime, don't I?" No place was going to be easy, but with her finances having dwindled to next to nothing, she couldn't afford to be off from work any longer. She needed this job to keep her life going.

"You're right. But please let me know when you need a break. Look at the schedule and make sure you give yourself adequate time off, not too many days in a row, okay?" Arlene gave her a sad smile. "You're a strong woman to have survived your ordeal, so I know coming back to work must seem a piece of cake after that."

Jeannine gave a small laugh. "Maybe not quite a piece of cake, but something I have to do. Starting over, starting fresh, is what I need right now."

During the interview process she had had to disclose why she had been out of work for so many months. She hadn't been on vacation for months at a time and she hadn't been terminated from her last job. A life threatening miscarriage had forced her to quit her job. Being a patient had given her a whole new perspective on life.

"There is a certain amount of difference between the ER and the ICU, so it may take some adjustment for you. Don't expect to learn everything at once."

"I won't. Moving from ER to ICU will hopefully give me a buffer. Never knowing what was coming through the doors in the ER was always stressful. I didn't realize how stressful until I left there."

"Well, in any case, I'm glad you're here." She nodded

toward the conference room. "Let's get in there before all the bagels are gone."

Jeannine grabbed half a bagel and found a seat in the back of the small room crammed with chairs. She nodded to staff members entering the room, but focused on the pastry in her hand.

When an amazingly handsome man entered the room, she nearly dropped her bagel on the floor. Tawny skin and dark hair that fell past his collar, he was broad shouldered and trim in the hips. She didn't know who he was, but he certainly commanded the attention of everyone in the room. With the long white labcoat, he was identifiable as a high-ranking physician at the hospital. Probably an attending physician or senior resident. She was too far away to read his name badge and several people shuffled past, blocking her view.

"Attention, everyone," Arlene said, and raised a hand. "Let's get started. You all know Dr. Kyriakides, I believe. But I want to introduce our newest staff member, Jeannine Carlyle. Jeannine, would you stand up?"

Reluctantly, Jeannine stood and choked down a bite of bagel that was suddenly lodged in her throat. "Hi, everyone," was all she could think of to say.

How lame is that? she asked herself, and sat again, wishing she could slide under the chair in front of her. But she soon forgot her embarrassment as the physician began his presentation of a pediatric case from a remote Indian reservation in New Mexico. Watching him, listening to the case history and the problems the patient had experienced during his hospitalization, Jeannine forgot for a short time that she was starting a new job, that her life had been completely uprooted, and simply lost herself in Dr. Kyriakides' voice and the slide presentation.

At the end of the presentation, staff members grabbed the remainder of the pastries and returned to their patients. Jeannine was the last to leave the room as the doctor packed up his computer. "Thanks for the presentation. It was very informative," she said.

"You're welcome. You're the new nurse, right?" he asked, and shook her hand.

The faint smell of his cologne drifted toward her, and she took a step back. "New at this job, but not a new nurse." Definitely not new to this game.

"Did you just move here or have you been in Albuquerque a while?" He finished rolling up the cables and stowed them in a black computer case.

"No, I worked across town. I needed a new start."

"That sounds serious. Starting over isn't very easy, is it?"

"No. It's not." Trying to avoid his piercing gaze was impossible. The dark hair and tawny skin gave him away as being of Mediterranean descent, but there was something else to him. Jeannine shrugged. He was none of her business except in a professional way. Beautifully exotic men were off limits to her. Relationships period were off limits to her, since the last one had almost killed her. "I…had a serious injury that took me out of work for a while, but I'm back in action now. Don't worry, Doctor, I'm up to it." Was she being defensive already? She didn't need to tell her life story to everyone she met today, did she?

"Worrying is wasted energy, as far as I'm concerned. And please call me Miklo. I know they like to toss the medical director title around a lot, but I'm a doctor just like the rest. I simply have more paperwork."

His engaging smile managed to pull her lips into an answering response.

"I'll try. I'm not accustomed to addressing physicians by their first names. Usually just the residents."

Miklo looked down at her and smiled. "Then just think of me as a really old resident."

Against her will, Jeannine laughed at the small joke. But laughing was something she hadn't done in some time and to be joyful on her first day at work was an unexpected gift. She'd learned to find those gifts in unusual places. "Thank you, Miklo." She stepped toward the door. "Guess I'll be seeing you later."

"Yes, well, welcome to University Hospital."

"Thanks," Jeannine said, and left the conference room.

Miklo watched the new nurse go. She was a trim, pretty woman with long blonde hair and blue-green eyes that were filled with pain. She'd said she was starting over, and he knew from his own painful experience that starting over was never easy, no matter the reason.

Life as he had known it had been changed by the death of his wife. Pregnant with their child, they had both died in a tragic car accident three years ago. He'd been working instead of taking Darlene to a baby shower. The grief, the guilt, burned within him still at unexpected times. Like now. Clenching his jaw, he shouldered the heavy computer case and left the PICU. With a quick glance down the hall, he saw Jeannine at the nurses' station with her head bent over a chart, a pair of reading glasses perched on her nose.

As he left the hospital and went about his day, the image of Jeannine at the desk stayed with him. She seemed to be a lovely woman, and he hoped that her transition was going to be a good one.

CHAPTER TWO

JEANNINE entered the PICU on her second morning to pure chaos. Eyes wide, she watched as Dr. Kyriakides argued with Arlene at the nurses' station.

"I need someone now."

"No one wants to go, and I won't force anyone," Arlene said. "You can't drag an unqualified nurse off to such a critical situation. It's just not safe."

"So you're going to let an injured child lie in an ambulance outside and do nothing about it?" Miklo asked. "Any nurse will do in this situation."

Arlene gasped. "That's not fair, Miklo. The ER is on divert. All the hospitals are on divert."

Jeannine stepped forward, uncomfortable but digging deep within herself, challenging the fear that always seemed to live in her lately. "What's the situation? I have ER experience." The lump remained in her throat, but she had to conquer her fear some time.

Miklo turned his blazing amber eyes on her. "Put your stuff down and come with me right now."

Jeannine handed her backpack to Arlene. "Will you hold this for me?"

"Jeannine, wait! I'm not sure you're up to this your second day here," Arlene said. "I know you wanted to get back into it, but it's too soon."

Miklo hesitated, looking between the two women. "Is she qualified or not?" he asked Arlene.

"Yes, but—"

He turned from Arlene and placed a gentle hand on Jeannine's back, propelling her forward with him. "Let's go. There's a child that needs us."

Barreling down the stairs together, they burst into the ER where staff raced back and forth, the intercom paged a physician, and the sound of muffled crying came from behind a curtain. "Where is—?"

"Let's try the ambulance bay. They were going to try to take him somewhere else, but in between the other hospitals went on divert, too." Miklo led the way to the ambulance bay.

Jeannine's attention was completely taken by the small, motionless patient on the gurney beside an ambulance. Miklo reached for the stethoscope that hung from his neck and listened to the little chest with a nod. "Chest seems okay." He looked at the paramedic, named Charlie, who stood on the other side of the gurney. "What do we have?"

"Male, approximately six years old, involved in an MVA with his mother, who is in the next ambulance." He looked at Jeannine. "You're in the wrong hospital, aren't you?" he asked.

Jeannine swallowed and gave him what she hoped

was a confident smile. "Oh, hi, Charlie. Nope. Moved over to the University Hospital just yesterday." One day on the job and she'd already been caught like a deer in headlights. Nothing used to stop her in her tracks, so this shouldn't either.

"Well, it's good to see you again," he said, and gave a quick grin. "The kid seems stable right now, but there's no telling what's under the dressings. There were so many abrasions and lacerations that we just put saline-soaked gauze on him."

"Good call," Miklo said.

Jeannine checked the IV bag to ensure the fluids dripped quickly through the line in his small arm. "Unwrapping his face is not going to be good, I'm suspecting," Jeannine said as she snapped on a pair of gloves and handed a pair to Miklo.

Sheree, the EMT at the head of the gurney, made a facial grimace. "I didn't want to try to intubate him in the truck, but he may need it." She squeezed the ambubag over the boy's face. "Right now he's breathing on his own, I'm just giving him extra puffs of oxygen."

"So far his oxygen level is okay," Jeannine said after a quick look at the monitor. "Heart rate is high, but not unexpected. Fluids are going in well."

"As long as his airway is stable, I'll hold off the intubation until he's under anesthesia. Let's have a look at him, and if he's stable enough we'll do X-rays and see what's going on under the wraps." Miklo reached for the blood-soaked bandages, then hesitated. "Can you get some sedation going?" Dr. Kyriakides asked Jeannine.

"Should we take him inside before we get started?" she asked. "I feel so helpless outside."

"There's no trauma room available yet, but there's a spare treatment room I know of down the hall," Charlie said.

"Let's move him there. Jeannine, I'll count on you to get the medications going."

"Okay. What do you like to start with?" Jeannine knew her heart was beating about as fast as the boy's, but adrenaline always flowed quickly during a crisis.

"Morphine." Dr. Kyriakides gave a quick visual scan of the boy, his gaze serious. "Looks about twenty-five kilos, so give him a morphine dose now with some midazolam for amnesia. We don't want him to remember any of this, if possible."

"I'll have to find the charge nurse first. I don't know where the medications are kept here," Jeannine said, and dashed toward the main desk. Minutes later she returned to the small room. With trembling fingers she began to push the meds into the IV tubing. "That ought to do it." Memories of those particular medications flowing through her own veins tried to push to the surface, but she held the memories at bay. In the midst of a crisis was not the time to remember her own recent trauma. She stroked the hair back from the boy's forehead. "Just be calm, we're going to take good care of you," she said to the unconscious child.

"Okay. Let's see what we have." Miklo's large hands gently peeled away the layers of bandages from the child's face. Fresh blood oozed from a multitude of cuts and abrasions on the boy's face and neck. Gently, Dr. Kyriakides opened the boy's eyelids and flashed a light into them.

"Pupils okay?" Jeannine asked as she went through the neuro checklist.

"Yes. I was looking for glass, but thankfully I don't see any," Dr. Kyriakides said. "Until we get X-rays, let's just leave the gauze on him."

"Okay. Do you think we should try Radiology right now or do you think they are as slammed as the ER is?" she asked. "He seems stable enough to transport, but I don't want to sit in X-Ray for an hour, waiting."

"Let me find out," Miklo said, and grabbed the phone in the room. After a brief conversation he hung up the phone. "They'll take us in ten minutes."

"Great. By the time we get him down the hall, they'll be ready," Jeanine said.

Miklo's strong jaw was tightly clenched and his firm lips compressed into a straight line.

"Doctor? Are you okay?" she asked, wondering if she was intruding on his thoughts.

Miklo turned to her and gave a slight smile. "I'm okay. Waiting for X-Ray makes me crazy sometimes."

"I know what you mean." She touched his sleeve, hoping to impart some comfort to him. Though he had said he was okay, she wasn't sure that was the complete truth. But, having just met him, she was not one to judge.

After multiple facial X-rays and a CAT scan to check for a brain injury, which was negative, the group took the patient straight up to the PICU since the ER had no space.

The boy started to wake up, and Jeannine took his hand. “Hi, there.” With her other hand she stroked his hair. All that was peeking out from beneath the bandages were frightened brown eyes that became wider with each breath he drew.

Miklo stepped away from the x-ray light box and returned to the gurney. “Hi. What’s your name?”

The boy glanced back and forth between Jeannine and Miklo without answering.

“Do you think he’s hearing impaired?” she asked with a frown. “I hadn’t thought of that.” Perhaps they had overlooked an injury to the middle ear, or maybe the boy was hearing impaired. Jeannine chewed on her lower lip, trying to think of all of the ways to communicate with him. “I didn’t see any ear injuries, but I suppose he could have sustained something in the wreck.”

“Let me try something first. *Ola. ¿cuál es su nombre?*” Miklo asked in Spanish.

Jeannine watched as the boy nodded and tried to speak. Her heart ached as he struggled to communicate, and remembered struggling with the same problem when she had woken up in a hospital bed unsure what had happened to her.

As she remembered her situation, an idea came to her. She rummaged around in a storage cabinet for a moment and returned with a paper printed with the alphabet. “Are you fluent in Spanish, Miklo?” she asked as sudden energy swirled within her.

“Yes.”

"Ask him if he can spell his name, and I'll hold up the chart."

Miklo relayed the information. The boy raised his hand and pointed to a series of letters on the communication board. *"¿Roberto? Su nombre es Roberto?"* Miklo asked, his voice soft as he spoke to the frightened child.

The boy gave a slight nod to verify his name. Jeannine grinned and was relieved to see the small smile Miklo gave her. "Brilliant. Now ask him if he can point out his phone number." With the mother still unconscious, they needed to find another immediate family member right away.

As Roberto pointed to the numbers, Jeannine wrote them down. "Chances are, whoever answers that number isn't going to speak English either. Do you want to make the call?" she asked Miklo.

"Sure. Why don't you go ahead and give him a little more sedation? He's probably wondering what's going on and right now I don't think we can tell him." Miklo's serious eyes continued to observe the boy.

Jeannine dialed the number and handed the phone to Miklo. While she listened to the rapid Spanish conversation, she added a few milligrams more medication. This sort of sedation ideally was figured in milligrams per kilogram of the child's weight. Right now they were giving a low dose, enough to keep him quiet but not enough to put him under completely.

Miklo hung up the phone. "The father's coming in." He bent over Roberto and relayed the information in a calm voice.

Jeannine watched as the man made soft eye contact with the boy. This was a man who cared about people. When she'd been hospitalized so many doctors and nurses had taken care of her that she'd lost track of their names and faces over the months. The sense of caring was one she carried with her to this day and motivated her to get out of bed every morning, hoping that she could give that gift to someone else.

Jeannine spoke to Roberto. "I know you can't understand me, but I'm going to take good care of you."

Miklo turned and translated softly as she spoke.

"I'm going to stay with you the whole way, okay?" she said, and gave him a smile.

Miklo watched as Jeannine spoke to the boy. She connected with her patients, that was obvious. But there was something about the way she spoke, the way her long fingers stroked Roberto's hair, and her gentle manner that spoke of compassion running deep in her veins. As if she understood what it meant to be on the other side of the gurney.

"I'm going to have to take him to surgery as soon as the dad signs the operative consent."

"I thought you were the medical director," she said.

"I am, but I'm also a maxo-facial surgeon." Miklo hesitated until Jeannine looked up at him. "I'm wondering if you would be able to accompany Roberto to the OR."

Jeannine blinked in surprise. "Me?" she squeaked. "I'm not an OR nurse."

"I know this is out of the ordinary, but I'm not asking you to perform the operation." Miklo gave a sideways smile. "He hasn't let go of your hand even under the sedation. Having a friendly face in the OR will go a long way to keeping his stress level down and my repairs in place."

Jeannine looked down at Roberto's gauze-covered face and then at the intensity in Miklo's. Could she refuse to help either one of them? "You're right. I know that having staff who care about you helps you heal faster." She was living testament to that. When her fiancé had fled in the face of her tragic illness, she had looked to her family, friends, and the nurses who had cared for her to get her through the worst of her crisis. She gripped the metal side rail with one hand. With her other hand, she touched the neck of her uniform.

"You sound like you have some personal experience in that arena," Miklo said, watching her with those dark, dark eyes.

Before she could answer, she was interrupted by frantic, rapid Spanish being yelled down the hallway. "I think the father's here," Jeannine said with a cringe.

"I'll get him." Miklo left the room and returned shortly with a hysterical man who spoke non-stop between sobs.

Miklo explained the situation to him, pointing out the problems of the facial injuries, the IV, and what the plan was. Jeannine produced a clipboard with the Spanish consent form, and the father signed it with a trembling hand. After returning the clipboard, he took a handful of tissues that Jeannine offered him. "*Estoy apesadumbrado,"* she said, one of the few Spanish phrases she knew, and she was sorry for his pain.

Miklo squeezed the man's shoulder in a gesture of support as he wiped his tears from his face. *"Gracias,"* he said, and shook Miklo's hand as well as Jeannine's. Tears gathered in her eyes as he struggled to control himself.

CHAPTER THREE

ROBERTO clung to her hand as Jeannine walked alongside the gurney to the OR. Images she tried to suppress of her own recent trips to the OR attempted to insinuate themselves into her mind, but she forced them back. Now was not the time for a trip down the memory lane from hell.

Miklo bent over the stretcher. He had quickly changed into OR scrubs and a bandanna-style head cover. Reaching into his pocket, he retrieved a toy race car and placed it in Roberto's hand, curving the little boy's fingers around it.

"What do you have there?" she asked.

"Just a little something for him to hold." Miklo shrugged and offered a quick smile. "I've found that children do better with some little token that they hold through procedures. Officially, it's called a transitional object, but I just like to call it a car." He shrugged, seeming to dismiss the idea.

Jeannine smiled. "That's a great bit of insight." She leaned over and stroked Roberto's hair back from the bandages on his face. "I should have thought of that."

"It's not a big deal," he said.

"Really, it is. Not everyone would go to such lengths to see to the comfort of their patients. Especially the little ones."

"It's just a toy car…"

"That will go a long way to keeping Roberto's stress level down." She looked at the little car clutched in the bruised fingers. "I could have used one myself not long ago."

Miklo watched as her mind seemed to wander a bit. What could she have meant by that comment? Observing the slight tremor of her hand, he guessed that it had something to do with the recent change in status she had alluded to yesterday. But it was none of his business. Getting overly involved with staff members' lives wasn't part of his job.

He had enough on his plate trying to live with the guilt that still plagued him daily. Taking care of patients and running his practice was all he could handle. Every time he handed a car to a child he was reminded of how he had failed in his life, how he had neglected his pregnant wife when she had needed him most, and of the child that would never be.

Jeannine's soft hand on his arm startled him from his haunted memory. Looking up, he met her concerned aqua gaze. "Sorry?"

"I said, 'Are you okay?'" she said, and removed her hand.

Miklo rubbed a hand down over his face. "Lost myself there for a moment. Let's get this boy inside, shall we?"

"Of course," Jeannine said, and watched as the man strode to the scrub sink.

After he turned away, a woman dressed in green scrubs approached Jeannine. "I'm Dr. Harrison, anesthesia."

"Hi. I'm a little lost as to what to do next," Jeannine said.

Dr. Harrison picked up a syringe and administered medication of some sort into the IV tubing. In seconds, Roberto was completely under. "He'll sleep now," Dr. Harrison said, and started to push the gurney down the hall. "Are you coming inside with him?"

"Dr. Kyriakides asked me to come along for emotional support." Jeannine didn't know quite how much support she was really going to be able to give Roberto, but she would try her best. No one should go through this situation alone.

"Well, he knows what he's doing, so if he's asked you along, there's good reason for it. Let's go inside and get him hooked up to my monitors."

They walked by as Miklo stood at the sink, performing his intensive hand and arm scrub. Even in simple green scrubs and a tied hair cover, Miklo would have commanded the attention of every woman in the area. The simplicity of his attire peeled away everything except the man. He didn't draw attention to himself intentionally, but something about him drew her to him, and she shivered, trying to resist the whisper of attraction that swept over her. Attraction was what had gotten her into trouble in the first place. She didn't need a repeat of that disaster.

As if sensing her gaze, or perhaps he had heard the gurney, Miklo turned toward her. His brown gaze met hers, and she held her breath for a second, startled at the intensity of his stare. He was serious, intense, and focused. Only a nod acknowledged her, but that simple gesture released her.

"Here. You can sit by me," Dr. Harrison said, and pulled a low stool beside her at the head of the bed. OR techs worked on setting up the sterile environment and covered most of the bed with large blue drapes. "Miklo will be close to us, but you'll be out of his way here."

"Thank you," Jeannine said, and sat, relieved to have something solid to hold her up.

Then Miklo entered, covered in sterile garb. He used his foot to scoot a low stool close beside Jeannine. Looking at her through the protective goggles, he gave her a wink of reassurance. "Are you ready?" he asked.

"Never further from it," she said, admitting her insecurity aloud. She'd discovered recently that admitting fears aloud often took the power right out of them. "I've had a lot of new experiences lately. What's one more?"

"Glad to hear it." Miklo looked at the rest of the staff members. "Everyone else ready?"

Nods all around seemed to satisfy Miklo, and he pulled the gauze away from Roberto's face.

Despite the gasp that wanted to escape her throat, she was fascinated by the whole operative process. "May I ask questions while you work or will it be too distracting?" she asked in a whisper.

"Ask away. This is a teaching hospital. If the doctors

don't teach something every day we're not allowed to come back," Miklo said without looking up.

This time she did gasp, and her eyes widened. "Are you serious?" she asked, then immediately bit her lip. She'd fallen for that one without even looking.

Miklo turned amused eyes on her for a second. "No. You seemed a bit tense. I just wanted to shake you up a little bit."

"Well, you certainly did that." She rubbed her nose and tried to calm the flutters in her stomach. "Just for that, you have to answer all my questions."

"Fire away."

Jeannine watched Miklo's gentle hands work their magic over Roberto's small broken face. Wires and pins were added to keep the fractures stable, but thankfully his little jaw didn't have to be wired closed. She asked questions through the procedure, but mostly watched. "This is just fascinating," she said.

"Make you want to be a surgeon now?"

"Hardly." She almost snorted. "Just gives me a greater appreciation of what you do. And of how fragile we all are."

After completing the last delicate suture, he snipped the end and turned to her. "Thank you, Jeannine."

A blush flashed over her face and neck. "You're welcome."

After six hours of surgery, Miklo was glad to be rid of the stifling sterile garb, and he took a deep, cleansing breath. Jeannine walked beside Roberto to the PACU, the post-anesthesia care unit, just outside the OR. Despite not being her area of expertise, she had held up well under the pressure of surgery.

"Are you okay?" he asked Jeannine, and touched her arm. Her skin was soft and he pulled his hand back, resisting the urge to let his hand linger there. Touching a woman had once been something he had done often every day, but since his wife had died, the urge to reach out had faded away.

"Yes, yes, I'm fine. That was just a marvelous experience. To see a case from start to finish is a fabulous opportunity. Thank you for including me." She stood beside Roberto's bed as the other nurses set up the monitoring equipment. "Should I return to the PICU or should I stay with Roberto?"

"I'll call Arlene and see if I can keep you here. When Roberto's recovered enough from the anesthesia, you can follow him back to the unit. It will be a well-rounded day for you then. He'll need to remain intubated for a while so that the stitches can heal a bit. The sound of your voice will be a comfort for him." The sound of her soothing voice was a small comfort to him, too, after such a long procedure. The rigors of surgery had always invigorated him until the last few years. Listening to Jeannine's voice during the procedure had somehow prevented that fatigue from overcoming him. Perhaps her presence wasn't a comfort to Roberto only.

"I never thought of my voice as a comfort, but I suppose it's the familiarity of it more than anything, isn't it?"

Jeannine touched her throat in a gesture of which she was completely unaware. Miklo followed the direction of her hand. He noticed a distinctive, tell-tale scar, and he frowned, his curiosity roused as he observed the pink tissue that hadn't fully healed. "You are quite right. Your instincts are very good for this sort of work."

"Will he continue to be sedated so he's not feeling choked by the tube?"

She dropped her hand, and he examined the scar as unobtrusively as possible. It was definitely a tracheotomy scar that marred the beauty of her otherwise flawless skin. "Yes. He'll have to stay in the PICU at least for tonight, possibly a few days, while he's monitored."

The look in her eyes seemed far off, as if she were looking elsewhere. Maybe she was. Who knew? And was it any of his business why she had a scar? Life was full of people who carried scars, inside and out. And he was one of them. With a mental sigh, he decided he needed something to distract himself from his thoughts. The direction they were headed wasn't going to be helpful for anyone. Work was his life, his passion, and something he needed to keep his black emotions at bay. Indulging in self-defeating behavior wasn't something he was going to do.

"Do you need a drink of water, or something to eat? For someone not used to surgery, it can be tough the first time."

"A cup of coffee would be wonderful." She flashed a smile. "And a bathroom break," she whispered, and crossed her eyes briefly.

Miklo almost laughed at her antics. He could appreciate her position. She hadn't had a break since she had walked in the PICU this morning. For that matter, neither had he.

"Come on. I need a cup of coffee, too." He glanced at the clock on the wall. "The canteen is open. Let's get lunch and have a real break. Roberto will be fine for a little while."

Since entering medicine as his father and three brothers had, he'd been focused on his career, with little time for anything else. Every beat of his heart revolved around the hospital. Time with family, stolen moments, and rare evenings off were cherished. Three years ago his family had picked him up from the most painful experience in his life. Now they seemed to have moved on, leaving him to his own devices. He knew it was his fault, but he couldn't seem to function outside his comfort zone of the medical world. This was his life and others depended on him. That's what he kept telling himself, what he needed to believe, or he would be on his knees from unimaginable pain and guilt. He had to believe that his time here was not wasted. That he hadn't sacrificed his family for nothing.

A group of four nervous-looking interns dashed past them on the way out of the canteen. One of them bumped Miklo's shoulder and brought him back to the present.

"I'll be right back. You go ahead," Jeannine said, and ducked into the ladies' room. In moments she returned with a smile lighting up her face. Finely arched brows over a pair of eyes the color of the sea, her smile seemed to shine just for him, and he took a quick breath.

"You were right, I needed this more than I realized." She filled a large disposable cup with coffee, added a little sugar and milk, stirred, then placed a lid on it. "Thank you."

"No problem." He fixed his own cup of coffee and followed her to the grill. After obtaining their orders, they sat at a small table and ate. Miklo took a few bites of his sandwich, then placed it on the plate.

"Not good?" she asked.

Uncomfortable with the question, Miklo shifted position. "I don't know how to answer that without sounding completely biased." He picked up the sandwich again, but didn't eat.

"Oh, do try," she said with narrowed eyes that sparkled with mischief.

He sighed and leaned forward. "Okay, so I'm half Greek, half Mexican. My uncle owns the best restaurant in town. After eating that kind of food all of my life, a simple sandwich from the hospital grill just doesn't cut it sometimes. Know what I mean?"

"I can appreciate your position, but as I've never eaten Greek food, I can't pass judgment on you." She took a bite of her sandwich, seemingly not bothered.

Miklo shot forward in his seat, incredulous. "Are you kidding? You've *never* eaten Greek food?" He leaned back and placed a hand over his eyes. "Woman, you have no idea what you are missing." He shook his head in amazement.

"Well, maybe some day you can show me." She laughed and took another bite.

"You're on," he said, just as his pager went off.

CHAPTER FOUR

"I THINK we're due back in PACU. And Arlene will think I've kidnapped you or scared you off completely."

"Oh, she knows it will take more than something like this to scare me off." Jeannine walked beside him as they returned to the PACU.

"You've been a nurse for a while then?" he asked, and held open the door to the stairwell.

"Yes. I think I've worn out fourteen pairs of nursing shoes in the last ten years."

"That's a lot of miles." He opened the doors to the PACU for her, his stride so long she had to lengthen hers to keep pace with him.

"I've heard someone say it's not the miles but the *mileage* that gets to you."

Startled by that insightful comment, Miklo sighed. "I'll go along with that," he said, thinking of the emotional mileage he'd incurred over the last few years.

"I'm sure you've put on a few miles yourself between medical school, residency and your hospital practice."

"Yes. Seems like I've been walking the same one over and over sometimes."

Before she could respond to that, they arrived at the PACU, and the friendly camaraderie between them faded a little. In this environment the expectations were different. She suddenly didn't feel as open with him as she had in the canteen when it had just been the two of them at a small table. Oh, well. Not a time to get curious about the medical director.

Two hours passed before the anesthesiologist declared Roberto responsive enough to be transported to the pediatric ICU. Jeannine assisted the PACU nurse to hook up transport monitors and together they moved him upstairs. Although Roberto was not under the influence of the heavier medications any longer, Miklo's instructions were to keep him slightly sedated.

Arlene appeared at the doorway of Roberto's room. "Jeannine, are you okay?" she asked, concern in her voice.

"Oh, yes. This has been a fabulous experience," she said, and placed a small blood-pressure cuff onto Roberto's arm.

"I was going to get angry with Miklo if he scared you off on your second day on the job." She moved closer and gave Jeannine a reassuring squeeze on the shoulder.

"You worry too much. Really. I sat through the operation and then had something to eat, so it's been a surprisingly good day."

"Good." Arlene placed a hand on her chest in obvious relief.

"What's good?" Miklo asked as he entered the small patient room. Everything in it was designed for children, and with Miklo's large presence everything seemed to shrink even more.

"Jeannine was just telling me you hadn't frightened her out of the job today, and I said that was good."

"She's been a trouper. But she kidnapped my patient," he said, and faced Jeannine.

"I did not! Dr. Harrison said he was able to go to PICU, so the PACU nurse called—"

Miklo gave a quick laugh.

"Miklo, stop teasing," Arlene said, and glanced at Jeannine. "You can sue him for harassment if you like. I'll be a witness." Arlene shook her head and left the room.

"You're not very nice to tease me so many times in one day, Doctor." Jeannine pulled out a clipboard with Roberto's chart and began to record his vital signs.

"I have to. Once you've been here a while you'll be too smart to fall for my little tricks."

Jeannine double-checked Roberto's IVs and the ventilator settings, made sure of the security of the tube in his mouth that assisted his breathing. Distracting herself from the appeal of Miklo was extremely important at the moment. Though she had recently suffered the biggest letdown of her life when her fiancé had deserted her, she suddenly found herself being pulled against her will toward Miklo. She mustn't allow herself to be drawn to him. That path only led to self-destruction. Once was enough for her.

"Jeannine? You got very quiet there for a minute. I

hope that I haven't offended you with my comments." Miklo took a step toward her, concern in his eyes. "I really was just teasing."

Jeannine swallowed hard as he reached up and removed the cover from his hair, allowing it to fall back over his collar. The dark, luxurious locks fell down in disarray that didn't impair his looks at all. The man was devastating to her senses, and he didn't even know it.

"No." She offered him a smile that was extremely lame. "I'm fine. Just been a long day, you know? Been a long day for you, too, I'm sure. Have anything fun planned for the weekend?" Jeannine asked and busied her fingers writing down vital signs she didn't really need.

"Me?" Miklo snorted. "Hardly." He held his hands out, indicating the area around them. "This is my life. Fun doesn't enter into it." Taking the stethoscope from around his neck, he listened to Roberto's lungs.

"I have a hard time believing that you don't have anything better to do than to hang around here all weekend. Don't have you have anything to keep you busy?" she asked. She had noticed the absence of a wedding band, but these days that didn't mean much.

"No." Now was not the time to tell her he'd given up his life for his family, entirely too late. "How about you?"

"I might get out and take a hike or go to an art show or exhibition. There's a bunch of stuff going on this weekend. You should try it."

"Thanks, but I'm more of a museum kind of guy."

"Really? Why is that?" Jeannine asked. He looked more like a museum guy than a craft show kind of person, but you never knew from looking at a person what they were like inside.

"You can sit in a museum and look at things that don't talk back to you and rarely have a crisis," he said, and picked up Roberto's chart.

"That's true, but I like being around people, too." Jeannine wasn't convinced by his philosophy. Sometimes people needed to interact with each other, rather than just watching life go by. Being alone for too long had made her desperate for company over the last six months.

Miklo rubbed the day-long growth on his face. He smiled a little crookedly in a gesture she was beginning to associate with him. His full mouth moved slightly to one side, but failed to form a complete smile. "My day doesn't end when the surgery does. There is always much more to do before I leave." Again he looked around them at the PICU.

"You'd rather go home and have a cold beer, right?" she asked.

Miklo laughed out loud. "You are exactly right. For tonight, though, I'll turn things over to the intensivist on call." He grabbed his labcoat from the back of the chair and headed toward the door. "Are you ready to go, too?" he asked, and paused at the doorway.

"Yes. I just need to give the night nurse report on what I've done, then I'll head out. Have a good night and it was a pleasure working with you today."

"Same here."

Jeannine gathered the chart and headed to the nurses' report room.

Just as she left, several family members came in to see Roberto. Miklo explained how the surgery had gone and what the boy's condition was. By the time he was through answering their questions, Jeannine had returned to the room. She gave Roberto's face one last stroke. "I'll be back in the morning," she said.

"Aren't you off tomorrow?" he asked, surprised that she would be working her first weekend on the job.

"I am, but I want to come in to see him anyway." She shrugged and looked away from his vibrant eyes. They saw way too much of the things she carefully guarded. Things that no one here knew about her.

"I'll walk you out, then," he said, and slowed his long stride to match hers.

They approached the front door of the hospital and emerged into the early evening twilight. The sun setting over the west mesa cast a muted peach glow low on the horizon. Not a cloud marred the distant sky for miles. Purple hues blended atop the other colors and melded into the approaching evening.

Jeannine cleared her throat and shifted her weight from one foot to another. "Well, good night, Doctor."

"Miklo, remember?"

"Yes. It's just hard to get used to change isn't it? I'm so used to addressing physicians by their titles."

"I wasn't always a doctor. Sometimes when I'm addressed as Dr. Kyriakides, I think people are talking to my father."

"Does your father practice here in Albuquerque?" she asked.

"Yes, but he's partially retired. Somehow he found the right balance between the obsession of medicine and having a life outside his work."

"But you haven't?" she asked, somehow feeling brave enough to ask the question of him.

"No," he said, and looked away from her. "I haven't."

"I'm sorry if I've probed too far, Miklo." She sighed, hoping she hadn't just ruined her work relationship with him by asking one question too many.

"It's okay." He turned to face her again, took a step forward, but hesitated. "You wouldn't want to go have that beer with me tonight, would you?" he asked, uncertainty in his eyes.

Surprised, Jeannine could hardly believe she heard him correctly. "Sorry?"

"I asked if you wanted to grab a beer with me. You're off tomorrow, I'm off duty now, and we could both use the break after the day we've had."

It was a reasonable suggestion, wasn't it? Just two co-workers relaxing together. "Sure, why not?" Jeannine said. The words were out of her mouth before she had time to think.

"How about Olympia's? It's my uncle's place and it's close."

"Sure. You know I've never been there, so I'm open to another new adventure today." There wasn't time to get used to one thing before she had another new thing in front of her today. But, then, there was no time to be scared or say no, was there?

"Why don't I drive and you can relax on the way

over?" he asked, and led her to his car. It was a sleek, silver Jaguar convertible.

Jeannine stopped short. "I don't think I can relax in a car like that."

"Come on, it's just a car," he said, and opened the door for her. But as she sank into the soft leather seat, she knew it was far from it. This was luxury like she'd never known or ever thought to indulge in. When Miklo folded himself into the vehicle, she shrank back a little, not accustomed to being so close to a man. Not for a long time. And not with someone as vibrant and alive as Miklo was. He breathed energy and life into everything he did. Being so close to someone who exuded that kind of energy was almost intoxicating.

He started the powerful engine and let it idle a moment before shifting into gear. They remained silent as Miklo maneuvered the car through the university area and found a parking place about a block away from Olympia's.

Jeannine stayed close to Miklo in the near dark of the street until they were in front of the Greek restaurant. "Ready?" Miklo asked.

Jeannine nodded.

He opened the door and allowed her to enter ahead of him. Somehow a table had been crammed into every available spot, but with enough room left for the troupe of dancers working their way around the room.

"Oh, my!" Jeannine said, and turned back to Miklo. His presence so close unnerved her, but she didn't know where to go inside. "I've never seen so many people in one place before," she said, practically shouting over the boisterous music and conversations. "This isn't against the fire code, is it?"

"Come on." Miklo grinned and took her hand in his as they worked their way through the crowd. "I forgot this is Greek Week at the university. It's absolute madness," he said close to her ear, and she shivered as his lips touched her skin. "Plus, it's Friday night. We'll find a spot, though."

Jeannine nodded as they plowed their way through the throng of people. She clasped Miklo's hand tightly, not wanting to lose him in the crowd. And she liked the feel of his hand tight around hers, the feel of his long fingers wrapped around her hand. A man hadn't held her hand in a very long time, and the gesture of Miklo keeping her close made her remember things long ago and best forgotten.

"Miklo! Over here!" An older gentleman wearing a white apron and waving a bar towel gestured them toward the bar. "How are you, nephew?" he asked, kissing Miklo on both cheeks and giving him a hearty hug. "You've waited too long to come and see me. Your auntie misses you, too."

"Yes, Uncle Seferino," he said. "But how could you have missed me with all of these people to keep you busy?" Miklo embraced the man with great enthusiasm.

"Oh, the heart knows, my boy. The heart knows," he said with a slight nod, and then his focus changed to Jeannine. Miklo introduced them. After welcoming Jeannine to his establishment, Seferino led them to the bar and squished two stools together. "Make room for my famous nephew, the surgeon," he said, and waved his hands to move people out of the way.

Though crowded, space opened up. Miklo assisted Jeannine onto a barstool and took the one beside her. He stiffened slightly as he brushed by her, and her fragrance filled his mind. Though the end of the workday, she smelled clean and fresh and very appealing. Squelching the sudden heat of desire down, he took a gulp of iced water that his uncle placed in front of him.

Uncle Seferino leaned over the bar. "What will you have, my dear?" he asked.

Jeannine glanced at Miklo. "We just came in for a beer."

"Bah! You can't survive on that, not with all the hard work you do," he said, and reached beneath the bar and pulled out two long-necks anyway. "Christo!" he yelled in the general direction of the kitchen. "We need food for your cousin Miklo and his nurse. Make them something."

Wide eyed, Jeannine reached for the beer and took a sip. Miklo reached for his as well, needing the refreshment the cold drink offered. "Don't worry. He's always like that." Speaking conversationally over the noise and music was impossible, and Miklo leaned closer to Jeannine to hear her response.

"I haven't been in this sort of crowd since college. I'd kind of forgotten how loud a place like this can be."

"Did you go to school here?" he asked.

"Yes, but I lived off campus. It was better that way. Not tempted to engage in much socializing."

"I didn't think that was possible in the first two years of college," he said.

"Well, I was very shy and very serious back then." She shook her head. It seemed like a lifetime ago.

"But not any more?" His gleaming eyes told her that he'd already formed an opinion about that.

"I've sort of…come out of my shell in the last year or so." Had been forced to was more like it.

Miklo glanced from her face down her body and then back up again. "You have a very nice shell."

CHAPTER FIVE

A SLOW heat burned inside her. Echoes of the past whispered through her, and she struggled to ignore them. Sudden tears formed in her eyes, and she blinked quickly, hoping that Miklo didn't see.

"I've offended you, haven't I?" he asked, and placed his warm hand on her arm.

"No. I'm just incredibly surprised." She reached for the beer and took another sip.

"Tears don't usually form because of surprise," he said, his breath hot in her ear.

Turning her face slightly, she was close enough to see tiny flecks of gold within the irises of his eyes that were framed by long, dark lashes. The shadow of a beard didn't make him any less appealing. His mouth was the most sensual thing about him. The way his lips moved, the way he formed her name, made her want to reach out to touch him in a way that was totally inappropriate. A way she was totally unprepared for, and she had to clench her fist to keep it in her lap.

Moistening her lips, she tried to get hold of her

senses. If she were a smart woman she would have pulled away from him at that moment. But his pupils dilated as his gaze lingered on her mouth. When he returned his gaze to her eyes, she saw questions in his eyes, the wondering, the hesitation, the hint of desire, and she couldn't move away from him.

She was definitely not a smart woman. At least not tonight.

All it would take would be moving half an inch forward and her mouth would be pressed against his. Her heart raced and her breathing caught tightly in her throat. Could she do it? Should she do it? Could she take that initiative and reach out to a man again? Or would she have her heart abused all over again?

Miklo's body tensed at Jeannine's close presence. She was so very appealing. She laughed, she didn't take herself too seriously, and she made his heart beat like it hadn't in way too long. This close to her, even in the middle of a crowded restaurant, he wanted to reach out to her, taste her lips and see if she was as sweet as she looked.

A dancer fell into Miklo's back, and he pitched forward, almost landing in Jeannine's lap. She clutched his shoulders to steady him. He grabbed the bar with one hand and her upper thigh with the other, easing his weight off her. "I'm sorry. Are you okay?" he asked, and tried to return to his seat. But he was too close to her. Too close to resist temptation any longer.

Before he could think better of it, he turned his face, opened his mouth over hers and pressed a kiss to her startled lips. A tangle of emotions raced through him as her soft mouth trembled beneath his. Though the kiss lasted for just a second or two, he felt the desire vibrate off her.

And then he was back in his seat, the crowded restaurant loud in his ears again, Jeannine's startled gaze on his.

"Did you just kiss me?" she asked, her eyes still wide with shock.

"I did."

"Why?" Now the shock turned to suspicion, and he didn't like that in her eyes.

"I don't know. I just wanted to." Indeed, he had.

She touched her lips with trembling fingers. "No one has kissed me in a very long time," she said.

"Me neither," Miklo admitted.

Jeannine flopped back against her chair. "Now, I find *that* hard to believe," she said, disbelief bright in her eyes.

"It's an unfortunate truth," he said, amused at her reaction.

"You work with a zillion nurses."

"Doesn't mean I kiss any of them."

"No, but surely you've been out with dozens of them, haven't you?"

"At one time, but that was long ago and far away." He took her hand and held it in his. He needed her touch, her warmth. He hadn't known he needed to be so close to another human being until now. He'd refused to admit he'd needed it for a long time. But he had once been a man who had laughed and loved deeply. And then his world had come crashing down around him.

"Miklo? What are you doing?" she asked, a husky tremor in her voice he heard even over the crowd, but she didn't pull away from his touch.

"There is something about you that makes me want to touch you, Jeannine. I don't know why, but touching you is a very pleasant experience."

"Until you see me naked," she said, and scoffed.

Miklo roared with laughter. "What makes you say that? I've seen plenty of naked women and haven't fainted yet."

She glanced down at their entwined hands. "My hands are about the only thing on me that's pleasing."

"Now it's my turn to say I find that hard to believe. You're a lovely woman, Jeannine. I'm sure every part of you is equally as lovely."

Adjusting her position, she couldn't hold his gaze for long and looked away. "I'm not terribly comfortable telling you this, but we'll be working together, so I'm sure you'll find out sooner or later." She drew in a deep breath. "My recent illness was a tubal pregnancy that almost killed me. That's why I have the trach scar. I was ventilated for a few months. My abdomen and chest are covered in scars from multiple surgeries, so are my arms. That's why you would run away screaming if you saw me naked." She shook her head. "I shouldn't have said anything. It doesn't have to interfere in our working relationship and won't affect my work performance."

"I'm not worried about that at all, Jeannine." He

moved one hand and brushed her hair back off of her shoulder. Her hair felt like silk. “But you seem quite bothered by the scars.”

“My fiancé left me because of them and the whole situation.”

“Then he was an idiot.” Dark anger simmered inside him. No one should be abandoned for such a reason.

Jeannine’s wide eyes clung to his. “No. He’s really a brilliant scientist.”

“But a very dumb man,” Miklo said. “If it will make you less self-conscious of the scars, I can take a look at them and see if there can be anything done surgically to decrease their appearance.”

“Then you’d really have to see me naked,” Jeannine said with a sad smile, and dropped her face into her hand.

“You only have to show me one scar at a time.” Putting her at ease was not going to be easy to do. But he had to try. Her scars likely went deeper than the surface, and she was telling him only part of her story. But if she wanted to tell him the rest, she would.

Pulling one sleeve up, she revealed a deep scar on her wrist about the size of a pea. “They’re all kind of like this,” she said.

In the semi-darkness of the restaurant, he couldn’t get a really good look at the scar, but he rubbed his thumb over it, learning its shape and texture. “This is from an A-line, isn’t it?” he asked, knowing that the monitoring device was inserted into the radial artery of the wrist. Long-term use created a divot in the skin that would never go away completely. "There are things that can be done to make the appearance less pronounced." Resisting the urge to lean over and kiss her wrist was difficult, but he managed to control himself.

"Here you go," Seferino said, interrupting the spontaneous examination. He set a steaming-hot plate of food on the counter between them. "Eat up!" Jeannine leaned back, and Miklo pulled away from her.

"We can't eat all that," she said, aghast at the amount of exotic-looking food on the plate. Foods she had never seen the like of before. "I don't even know where to start."

Napkins were piled up beside the dish, but no utensils. "It's all finger foods, don't worry. This is *spanikopita*, this is *dolmeh*," Miklo said, and pointed out the different items and picked up one with his hand. "Stuffed grape leaves," he said, and took a bite. He stifled a groan and motioned for her to try it.

"What's it stuffed with?" she asked, and cautiously reached for one.

"Lamb, rice, spices, and I don't know what else, but it's great." He took another bite. "And he makes the best *taquitos*, too."

Jeannine took a small bite of the *dolmeh*, her mouth coming alive at the mixture of exotic tastes in her mouth. It was tangy and wonderful and made her mouth water for more. "You're right. This is fabulous."

"See? Didn't I tell you? Now aren't you sorry that you've never tried Greek food?"

"I am," she said, and reached for another morsel. "You may never get me out of here."

They had been at the restaurant long enough that the crowd had started to thin, the dancers had finished, and the volume of music had been turned down. Conversation between them was easier now.

"Jeannine, I have to say you did great today. Thank you for agreeing to help out. I don't know what would have happened if you hadn't showed up when you did."

"If it hadn't been me, someone else would have helped out. I didn't do anything special."

"You heard Arlene. No one else was willing to go." He shook his head. "I'm rather disturbed by that. No one wants to go, sure, but when there's a crisis we all need to pull together and help out." The intensity of his eyes made her pause. "You shouldn't have had to go today, but I'm very glad you did."

"Things work out the way they are supposed to sometimes." As she said it, she thought of her ex-fiancé. Perhaps they hadn't been as well suited as she had once thought, and the end of their relationship had been the way things were supposed to be. Maybe she just wasn't cut out for a long-term relationship, family, or children.

"Some nurses don't do well outside their special area, but you did fine."

A blush stole over her face and neck, coloring her pale skin. "I was kind of afraid at first, but after a while it didn't seem so intimidating. Your attitude helped a lot to keep me calm."

"You didn't appear intimidated at all, even though you were out of your element in the OR and PACU. You did a great job with Roberto."

"Thanks," she said, and met his gaze with a shy smile. The effect of her blue-green gaze on him was instantaneous. His body flared, suppressed desire flashed to life within him. Something electric passed between them. Something he hadn't experienced in a long time. Something more than loyalty or honor, with a hint of a passion that lingered beneath the surface. Something that intrigued him. Something that he wanted to explore.

Was it just shared camaraderie, shared concern for a traumatized little boy, or was there something else going on? "You have the most amazing eyes," he said, and felt suddenly foolish for speaking aloud. Those eyes turned up at the outer edges, and Miklo had the sudden urge to hold this woman against him. In the midst of a crowd, in a totally inappropriate way, but he ruthlessly checked that urge. It would only lead to disaster for both of them. That was something that neither one needed. His life was not about pursuing a co-worker or getting romantic in any way. Jeannine deserved someone who could give her everything a man was supposed to give a woman. He'd already failed a woman once. He didn't want to fail another, especially after what Jeannine had been through with her fiancé. She didn't need that.

Looking away from him, Jeannine drank from her beer. "So, tell me. You are fluent in Spanish. Are you fluent in Greek as well?"

"Yes. I also speak Italian and a bit of Portuguese." The change of subject was a relief. Neutral topics were safest for both of them.

"Wow, I'm so jealous. My Spanish is limited primarily to *donde está la margarita?*"

Miklo nodded. "It's a good phrase to remember, though." Then he frowned. "You spoke a little in Spanish today, didn't you?"

"Yes, but my Spanish is basic at best. I took a class in medical Spanish once, but don't remember much."

"If you like, I can give you a few key phrases that would be helpful."

"Oh, that would be great. I should dig out my notebooks from that class and brush up again. I meant to do that while I was on leave, but never was able to get around to it." Was she going to do that just to impress Miklo or was she really doing it to help her patients? Sitting here with Miklo, she didn't really know. But in either case her patients would only benefit.

This atmosphere, the food and music, were so foreign to her, yet she began to relax more than she had in months. She'd been raised in a very conservative home and taught that to eat with the hands was improper. But right here, right now, seated close beside Miklo, it seemed perfect. He seemed right at home, and she was determined to step out of her comfort zone, even if it was just with a simple plate of food. Remaining in her comfort zone had become a way of life and not one that necessarily enhanced it. Now, in the span of one shift at work, her ideas of comfort had been changed.

Just as she was about to reach for another bite, Miklo's cellphone rang, and he pulled it from his pocket. In a broken conversation all she could glean was that there was trouble at the hospital. He snapped the phone shut and grabbed her arm. "Let's go. Roberto's in trouble."

CHAPTER SIX

IN WHAT seemed like seconds, they were out of there, racing the few short blocks to the hospital. "Did they say what was wrong?" Jeannine asked, trying not to think of the worst-case scenario.

"Respiratory distress. He's fighting the tube, and the nurse is afraid to sedate him much more than she already has without me being there. We need to see what's going on." He raked a hand through his hair. "I knew I shouldn't have left. If something happens, I'll never forgive myself." Add that to the list of things he was guilty of.

Jeannine didn't like the sound of that statement or the grim set of his jaw. "You need a break sometime, Miklo. That's reasonable. You said your father found a balance between work and life—can't you do the same? Surely there's an intensivist in the ICU at all times, isn't there?"

"It's Friday night. You know what it's like. There's no one who is as experienced as I am with this sort of facial trauma." Mouth compressed into a tight line, Miklo hurried them into the hospital.

A crowd had gathered around the bed where Roberto lay, his eyes wide and panicked, his arms and legs thrashing with every breath he took. "Everybody, back. Give the kid some room," Miklo said, and then spoke softly in Spanish to Roberto.

Jeannine heard the strain in his voice, knowing he needed to take command of the situation without panicking Roberto in the process. Approaching Miklo from behind, she whispered, "What kind of sedation do you want me to get?"

"Come round to the other side of the bed. I want him to hear your voice first. Let him know you're here. That will probably calm him more than anything else," Miklo said, and Jeannine did as he instructed. "It's more important for you to be at his side right now."

He turned around to the PICU nurse assigned to Roberto and gave her orders for sedation.

"Will you translate for me?" she asked as she looked down at Roberto.

"Yes, of course."

Jeannine took a breath and looked at Miklo. Faced with helping a child or saving her own pride, she knew she had no choice. What she was about to say could put her in a very awkward situation with Miklo, having him know more about her past than she was comfortable with. None of her coworkers knew what she was about to reveal.

"Roberto, you must not fight it," Jeannine said, and Miklo began the translation, his voice soft as he turned her words into what Roberto could understand. "It's not going to hurt you. The tube is to help you breathe better, and if you fight it, it won't work right. I had one once, and I know it feels bad, but try to close your eyes and not think of it. Think of the new little car we brought you." She produced the blue car from beneath his pillow where she had stowed it earlier. "The feelings in your throat will go away, and in a few days you'll be able to talk again. I know it chokes right now. It choked me, too, but it's only for a little while. Try to relax, and let the machine breathe for you. Don't fight. Don't fight it." She gave him a smile. "Just relax. Just relax."

Miklo watched her as she spoke from her heart. She stroked Roberto's head and kept her voice calm. Roberto's heart had been racing, but now the monitor showed it was slowing to a more normal level. The ventilator that had been struggling to keep up with Roberto's erratic breathing no longer alarmed. Roberto's eyes were wide open and intently focused on Jeannine's face.

"He's listening to you. Keep talking," Miklo urged.

Jeannine gave a smile and nodded. "You're doing great. Pretty soon all of this is going to go away, and you'll be back to playing again. Pretty soon nothing will keep you from having fun. This is just for a little while so that your stitches can heal," Jeannine looked at the other nurse. "Has his father been in?"

"No. He's still with his wife. She's critical. But there are other family members in the waiting room. Can we get one of them to come sit with him?"

Jeannine focused on Miklo. "Can we get his dad

over here to visit for a little while? Roberto needs to know his family is out there. He needs to know someone he loves is nearby."

"Sure. If his family is anything like mine, there are fifty people out in the waiting room and they aren't going anywhere. Maybe one of them can stay with Roberto's mother for a while."

"I have the sedation, Doctor," the other nurse said, pausing at the end of the bed. "Are you still going to want it?"

"Yes. The crisis is over for the moment, but in order to avert another one, I think it's best to keep him under. I'll write up a more liberal regimen in a few minutes. Don't be afraid to use it."

"The nurse is going to give you some medicine to make you relax some more," Jeannine said. "It's going to feel like butterflies are all around you, and when you wake up, you'll feel better again." She took a deep breath, remembering the butterflies that she had experienced when she had been a patient in the ICU. "Do you have pain?" she asked. Roberto frowned and tears overflowed his expressive brown eyes.

"Miklo, can you add some extra pain medicine and throat spray to that cocktail? When I was intubated, it was the worst feeling of my life," she said, and swallowed roughly and touched her neck again.

"Absolutely." He again translated the information to Roberto and added to the orders for the ICU nurse.

As soon as the nurse administered the medication, Roberto's eyelids started to droop. Jeannine held his slack hand in hers for a few more minutes. "He's exhausted, poor guy."

"It's been a long day for us all," Miklo said with a sigh.

"I'm sure you're more exhausted than anyone else. You're not on call tonight, too, are you?" she asked, hoping he would get to go home.

Though his days ended, his nights seemed to go on forever. "No, but I'll probably just crash in one of the on-call rooms in case he has trouble again." Sleeping in the call room wasn't ideal and brought back too many memories of the night his family had died. He'd been on call then, and had been powerless to save his wife and child. "Come on. You've done enough for today. Why don't I walk you out to your car?"

Jeannine took a deep breath and rubbed a hand over her face. "I think I'm ready to call it a day." She sighed and placed Roberto's hand by his side with the little car against his palm.

"I'll be back in a little while," Miklo said to the ICU nurse. "We need to avoid another event like that one."

"Yes, Dr. Kyriakides," she said, and turned back to the monitor.

"What do you think caused his trouble? Just anxiety?" she asked as they made their way to the back of the hospital and out to the parking lot.

"Yes. As you say, the tube is quite uncomfortable, though I don't have the same familiarity with it that you do." He followed her to a small red car.

"How long do you think he has to have the tube in?"

she asked as she opened the door to the car and stowed her belongings on the passenger seat.

"Another day, possibly two." He shrugged, and then he looked at her, giving up on subtlety. "You've been through a difficult time, haven't you?" He wanted to reach out and push the hair back from her face, but he resisted the temptation. If he touched her again, he wasn't sure he'd want to stop.

"Yes," she whispered, and tried to hold at bay the boiling emotions inside her. "Talking to Roberto has brought back a lot of things I'd rather have forgotten about. But if I can put my feelings aside and help someone else, then I'm happy."

"That can't be all you want out of life, is it?" he asked. "There has to be more to you than your work."

"I could turn that question back to you, Doctor."

"Touché. It's none of my business. But the way you care about people and the passion you put into your work is really very inspiring." Something he hadn't felt in a long time. Something he desperately needed in his own life, but didn't know how to find it. Something he never expected to want again. Until now. This was a day full of surprises all round.

The sadness returned to her eyes, and he didn't like the dark circles under them, but knew they were well earned today.

"Well, goodnight, Miklo," she said, and curved a hand behind her ear, pushing her hair back. "It's been a very interesting day."

Miklo laughed and some of his fatigue eased. Before

he could think better of it, he kissed her on both cheeks. Something inside him couldn't or wouldn't prevent the gesture. She needed it, and for some reason he wanted to be the one to give it to her. Her gasp of surprise pleased him.

"For someone who claims not to have kissed any nurses recently, you're doing quite a lot of it today." She narrowed her eyes playfully at him, considering him suspiciously.

Miklo laughed, liking the feeling of it rolling through his chest and his heart. Focusing on her again, he stepped closer. "You're right about that."

Jeannine's cautious gaze held his. He could see the hesitation in her, the frown of worry that flitted across her brow. And he waited. Any moves made right now were going to be hers. But if she moved toward him, he certainly wasn't going to stop her.

"In the restaurant, when you kissed me?" She licked her lips once and chewed on the lower one, hesitation and uncertainty in every move she made.

"Yes?"

"It was very nice."

"Nice? It was just *nice?*" Dumbfounded, he stared at her, trying not to be insulted to the depth of his manhood.

"Very nice. In a totally hot way," she rushed to assure him. "But it was so quick I didn't have time to make a full assessment." Her hands touched his chest and rested lightly there, warmth pulsing from her palms into him.

"I see." Looking down at her, he eased closer, his

hands reaching out to draw her in. "So would you like another to be sure of your initial impression?"

"Yes," she whispered a second before she closed the gap between them and kissed him.

Miklo's arm close about her waist held her tight against him. Without thinking, she locked her arms around his shoulders and held him full against her. Miklo ravaged her mouth with his, his tongue, his lips, his teeth, everything together assaulted her senses. Thank God she was leaning back against her car or she would have melted to the ground. She'd never been held by a man like Miklo. She'd never been so thoroughly devoured by a kiss.

Jeannine surrendered to the moment and gave herself to Miklo's heat. Only after being turned to mush did Jeannine pull away from him. Both of them breathed heavily. Miklo turned and leaned back against the car beside her and caught his breath.

"So, was that to your liking?" he asked.

"Oh, yes. I think that'll do," she said, trying not to humiliate herself in front of him. She had felt that kiss all the way to her toes, and her lips still tingled.

"Seriously, Jeannine. I've enjoyed spending time with you today. And I've never taken a nurse to Olympia's or kissed one in the parking lot."

"I see. So this is a one-time deal, then?" she asked, unsure how she really felt. The day had been unnerving in so many ways.

"I didn't say that. I'm simply explaining that...there's something about you that has inspired me today."

"I'm feeling much the same. I haven't been attracted like this for some time." Why, she couldn't say, but attraction like this was something she'd never experienced, even with her fiancé. Theirs had been a more cerebral relationship. Something inside of her had sprung open today.

Pushing away from the car, he opened the door for her, and she slid inside. "I'll see you soon," he said.

"Good night." She drove off with a casual wave. He watched until she safely left the parking lot, and then made his way back to Roberto's bedside, wondering why Miss Jeannine Carlyle had intrigued him so deeply in less than one day.

CHAPTER SEVEN

THE next morning Jeannine stood in the doorway of Roberto's ICU room and caught her breath. The two cups of steaming coffee started to burn her hands as she stared at Miklo.

He sat in a recliner with his arms crossed over his abdomen, his feet up on another chair, and he was fast asleep. His chest rose and fell with the rhythm of his breathing. More than likely he'd spent most of the night sitting up with Roberto, and her heart went out to him. Dedicated doctors never caught a break. He had to be exhausted after the day they'd had, and then a night sleeping in a chair on top of that. In her own bed, she'd slept like a rock. Here, she wasn't sure how he could have slept propped up like that.

After setting the cups on the counter, she focused on Roberto. Quickly assessing his condition, she noted his skin was flushed and his heartbeat was too fast for her liking.

Jeannine touched the back of her hand to the side of his neck.

"Is he still hot?" Miklo asked, his voice husky and rough.

Turning, Jeannine saw that Miklo hadn't moved. "How did you know I was here?"

"Coffee. I can smell it all the way over here."

Jeannine grinned, then hid her expression. "I figured you could use some of the good stuff this morning."

"Thanks," he said, and stretched, then stepped closer to Jeannine, and her heartbeat fluttered just about as fast as Roberto's. "His temp started climbing a few hours ago. I started an antibiotic that will hopefully cover any bacteria he might have been exposed to."

"Infection goes hand in hand with any trauma, doesn't it?" An unfortunate truth. Trauma wounds always came in dirty.

Jeannine bit her lip and pushed Roberto's damp hair back from his face. His tawny skin seemed pale, and she pulled down his lower eyelid to examine the color of the inside.

She turned to Miklo. "What are his labs like today? He seems pale to me."

"Good observation. He's a little low on the blood counts. It's hard to say how much blood he lost already, and then we've diluted it more with the IV fluids. But if he drops any more, he might need a transfusion." Having a nurse with such insight and ability to think through the medical issues of a patient was certainly an asset to have in any situation. Though there were plenty of experienced nurses in the pediatric ICU already, she was certainly going to be an asset.

Jeannine glanced away from him and picked up a cup of coffee, fiddling with the lid and adjusting it. "Well, I guess I'll go now." She shrugged. "I just wanted to check on him. Enjoy the coffee."

As she walked away, Miklo had a sudden urge to convince her stay. Or go with her. Or…something. Taking a step toward her, he hesitated. "Jeannine?"

She turned to face him, her delicate brows lifted, opening her blue-green eyes wider as she waited for him to speak.

Now what was he supposed to do? Think of something clever to say? *That* was out of the question. He'd run out of clever a long time ago. He cleared his throat and frowned as he struggled to make the right words come out of his mouth. "What are your plans for today? Got anything going?"

"Well, there's a new exhibit at the Museum of Natural History I was going to check out." She hesitated for a second. "If you don't have plans, I wouldn't mind the company," she said, then clamped her mouth shut.

"Change your mind already?" he asked, amused at her reaction. At least her reactions were honest, and she didn't try to hide them.

"No." Gave him a sideways look that clearly said she was thinking about it. "When you're around, I just seem to say whatever comes into my mind."

"That's okay. I like your spontaneity, and I'd love to come." He walked to Roberto and spoke a minute to him, then grabbed his labcoat from the back of a chair. "I'll change and meet you in the lobby in ten minutes."

Soon after, they were driving away from the parking lot of the hospital toward the Old Town part of Albuquerque, settled in 1706. Though primarily geared to tourism, Old Town boasted a number of great museums and restaurants. "It's a gorgeous day, isn't it?" he asked, trying to fill the silence that seemed to have settled between them.

"Yes. I love days like this. Clear blue skies, not too hot, and little humidity. Perfect to me." She looked up at the sky overhead and as she leaned back against the seat, the scar he had noticed yesterday appeared above her collar.

"Well, if the weather holds, maybe we can have lunch *al fresco*." He used to spend a lot of time outside hiking or biking, but his life of late hadn't allowed much time for recreation. It was simpler if he just worked.

"You sound so Continental when you say that," Jeannine said, and gave a quick laugh. "I've never been out of the States, but I want to someday. I have a passport, but I've never used it. That's so lame, isn't it?"

"Not even on spring break from college?" he asked, truly surprised. Everyone he knew traveled. As a child he'd traveled to Greece three times before he'd been ten years old.

"Nope. Back then I was painfully shy and didn't know what I really wanted out of life." She turned toward him, her face serious.

"That's what college is for, figuring out who you are and what you want." He shook his head, remembering his own recklessness as a student. Those days were long gone and frivolity not something that was a part of his life any longer.

"My college experience was a little more conservative than that."

"So do you know now who you are and what you want out of life?" he asked.

Jeannine thought for a moment. "Sometimes I do and some days I just don't."

"You need to go back to college, then," Miklo said with a laugh.

"Hey!" Jeannine said. "That's not fair. Some people don't know what they want to be when they grow up until they're, like, thirty. I suppose you have it all figured out, then, Dr. Kyriakides?"

Sobering, Miklo negotiated the narrow streets until he found the parking lot by the museum. "I thought I had once but, like you, some days I'm not so sure." He snorted and turned the engine off. "Maybe I need to go back to college, too." Without another word he opened the car door, came around and opened her door for her.

"Let's go see some dinosaurs," she said, and smiled up at him.

"Good plan," Miklo said, and walked silently beside her.

They continued without speaking again until they made their way through the first exhibit of dinosaurs. They gazed through the glass at a museum worker who was tediously cleaning a dinosaur fossil by removing the rock it was encased in, one speck of dirt at a time. Long moments passed as other museum-goers stopped to watch the work being done. The people made comments, and drifted away to other areas of the museum.

"Any lingering issues from yesterday?" he asked as they moved to the next exhibit.

"Well, I'm pretty certain I don't want to be a surgeon, like you," she said.

"At least that's one decision you came to without having to go back to college."

"See how helpful you are?"

"Seriously, Jeannine. If you have anything you'd like to talk about, I'll try to help." He sighed and guilt crashed over him. "I had no idea you'd been through a recent hospitalization. If I had I could have—"

"It's okay, Miklo." She touched his arm and the warmth of her hand was gentle on his skin. Instead of comforting her, she offered it to him with a small smile. "I learned a lot yesterday. I've come to realize that learning opportunities are not always as easy and pleasant as yesterday was."

"If I had just known…" But he had been thinking of his patient, not himself, not the staff. The same way he'd been thinking of his patients and not his family the night they had died. God! He was so stupid sometimes, so focused, so…blind.

"Actually, it was a good thing for me to do. I didn't have time to think about it, and working with Roberto gave me a chance to stretch my wings as a nurse again. I haven't pushed my boundaries for a long time."

Miklo gave her a sideways smile, admiring the guts

it had taken for her to walk into that OR yesterday. "You are definitely one of the bravest people I have ever met." Her courage humbled him, and it was something he obviously needed a large dose of now and then.

"Me? No way. I can't even get on an airplane without having an anxiety attack. I'm like one of those people you see on the commercials, hyperventilating into a paper bag."

Miklo laughed and it was good to feel the sensation rumbling through his chest again. "Then I guess going flying with me in my plane this afternoon is out of the question."

She gave him a look of astonishment. "Absolutely."

Though fear flashed in her eyes, the slight smile that curved her full lips upward made him think there might be another time for her to fly. "Come on, then, let's go see the rest of the dinosaurs." Miklo took her hand in his.

It seemed the most natural thing in the world to have Miklo's hand clasping hers as they wound their way through the prehistoric exhibits, chatting about nothing in particular. Then they were seated to watch the IMAX film on a two-story screen designed to draw the viewer in and almost become part of the show.

Jeannine lost herself in the sights and sounds of the undersea adventure, but lost herself more in the feel of Miklo's arm warm and comforting around her shoulders. The longer the film progressed, the more she relaxed into him, his arm tucking her against his side. The hesitation in her lifted, and she rested her head against him. In the dark he couldn't see her scars or feel their rough texture. The dark setting gave her a certain amount of freedom that she never would have otherwise found.

With a sigh, he rested his chin on the top of her head. Jeannine closed her eyes and listened to the beating of her heart. Somehow, she had never heard it beat the way it did now, filling up every void in her body. Each breath she took filled her with hesitant joy and Miklo's spicy scent.

Then he pressed a chaste kiss to her temple, and the moment froze as one she would never, ever forget.

No man had ever made her feel this way. Whatever it was in Miklo that she found attractive seemed to have settled deep within her, and wasn't going to go away. The thought aroused and frightened her at the same time.

He turned slightly toward her and the warmth of his hand cupping her cheek caught her off guard. She couldn't see his eyes, but she felt the intensity of his gaze as he guided her face up to his. Desire that she hadn't allowed herself to feel unfolded inside her, one delicious petal at a time. Could something that felt so delicious be wrong? She was about to find out.

Unable to deny the thoughts, the feelings, and the need hurtling to the surface, she gave in. The memory of his kiss from last evening raced through her and with it the desire for more. Raising her face, she leaned toward him, searching for that connection, that fulfillment it seemed that only Miklo could offer.

She wasn't disappointed. With his mouth a hair's

breadth from hers, he breathed in, seeming to inhale her scent, her fragrance, her essence into himself. A tremor shot through him that rebounded in her as he lowered his head and took her mouth with his.

The shock of electricity created by his warm mouth lit fires deep within her. A moan that had been trapped within her rumbled free, and she clung to Miklo, needing the taste of his tongue, the heat of his mouth, and the desire of his body to make her once again feel like a woman. The last man to touch her had made her feel worthless. Miklo made her feel delicate as he held her against him.

He didn't know why he did it. Was it the story she had told about her injury, the details she'd left untold, or was it the nuance of attraction he'd felt for her from the start? Whatever it was, he didn't want to think about resisting it.

As her soft lips parted beneath his, he knew he wanted to hold her, fold her against him, and not let her go for a very long time. She tasted both sweet and salty, like the popcorn they had sampled earlier. Her hand on his neck made his heart race and he delved deeper into her mouth, exploring, tasting the heady rush that sprang into him.

A scream ripped through the theatre, and they sprang apart. "What the…?" he said as another scream rang out, this time for help.

"Something's wrong." Jeannine stood and tried not to lose her balance in the narrow walkway between the rows of seats. "Stop the film!" She waved her hands at the attendant, who didn't immediately respond. "Stop the film!"

"Help! My husband's having a heart attack!" a woman cried.

The lights blazed on. Miklo and Jeannine weren't the only ones on their feet. "Who's calling for help?" he shouted.

"Over here," the attendant yelled, and waved her hands at them. "Over here!"

Miklo climbed straight up over the rows of seats to reach the ill man, and Jeannine raced around the row and back again.

As soon as he saw the man, he knew they were in serious trouble. He looked at Jeannine and saw his own assessment in her eyes.

"Call 911," they said in unison. The attendant raced off.

Miklo knelt beside the elderly man who perspired profusely, his hand clutched to his shoulder and his eyes were wide with panic. Reaching for the man's pulse in his neck, Miklo clenched his teeth. "He's probably in V-fib."

"Do you have any medical equipment?" Jeannine asked the manager, who had hurried in.

"Yes, but it's only for trained personnel."

"We're trained personnel. Get it in here," she said, and turned to Miklo. "Do you have your medical bag in your car?"

"Yes, but what I have is limited," Miklo said, his voice quiet and calm, instilling the same in her. "If they have a defibrillator we're going to have to shock him. He's not responding to carotid massage."

"Cough. Cough really hard," Jeannine instructed as the man's eyes drooped. "Stay with us. Now cough hard!" She shook his arm, trying to keep his attention focused.

The man made a weak attempt to do as she instructed, but he could no longer respond.

"He's going out," Jeannine said, and caught his head as he lost consciousness.

CHAPTER EIGHT

"LET'S get him to the floor," Miklo said and together they struggled to get the man out of his seat and onto a flat surface.

"Here's everything," the attendant said, and set the equipment beside them.

"I'll start CPR. I hope you remember your algorhythms for adults," Miklo said. "One…and…two…" Miklo gave the cadence for the compressions. Jeannine used the breathing mask to administer oxygen to the man at appropriate intervals.

"I took my ACLS over again last month, so I'm good," she said, knowing that this man's life depended on her correct interpretation of a code situation. "Thankfully they have a defibrillator. Let's do a round then check his rhythm."

They worked on the man as his wife stood by and wept. What seemed like hours later, paramedics arrived, but it was actually no more than ten minutes. With the extra help, they worked to stabilize the man. After two defibrillation attempts, the man hadn't responded.

Jeannine sat back on her heels, a frown between her eyes as she watched Miklo's determined face. The intensity almost sparked off him. If he wasn't giving up, neither was she.

"Let's try one more shock," she said, and looked up for Miklo's nod of agreement. "Come on, you can do it. Stay with us, stay with us," she mumbled aloud. "Charging paddles." In seconds the whine of the machine indicated full charge. "Everyone clear." She pressed the paddles to the man's chest and discharged 360 joules.

Agonized seconds passed as they stared at the monitor. And then his heart beat again in a steady rhythm across the screen. Jeannine breathed a huge sigh of relief and sat back on her heels again. Her arm and leg muscles screamed from the exertion. She wasn't used to this type of activity.

The paramedic gave the patient more oxygen, mimicking a respiratory pattern. "He's not breathing yet, but at least we have a rhythm," he said. "Excellent job, guys. Excellent."

Miklo panted from his exertions and wiped the sweat from his face. "Let's get him packed up and to the hospital. I'm not sure he'll be stable for a while."

"Got it," the paramedic said, and loaded the man onto the stretcher.

Jeannine used the seat to pull herself up and stood on shaky legs. She hugged the man's wife as the woman gained control over her emotions and stopped sobbing. "Will you be okay to drive to the hospital by yourself?"

"Yes. I'll call my daughter to meet me there," she said, and pulled out a cellphone. "Thank you. Thank you both so much. If you hadn't been here I know he would have died." She gave Jeannine a desperate hug.

Jeannine didn't voice her concern that the man wasn't out of trouble yet, but hugged the woman back, hoping to give her some confidence. "You be careful and drive slowly to the hospital. The guys will take good care of him until you get there."

The woman nodded and rushed out the door after the stretcher.

Applause erupted in the theatre as Jeannine and Miklo looked up in surprise. Jeannine blushed, and Miklo grinned. He put up a hand and acknowledged the appreciation of the people surrounding them. Jeannine was astonished at how calm he appeared. She was still shaking all over and she wasn't sure her legs would hold her up much longer.

"Had enough of the museum for one day?" he asked with a sideways grin.

The comment took her off guard, and she laughed. "I believe I've had enough for one day." Jeannine gathered her purse from beneath her seat and they exited the theatre back into the main museum. "After all that excitement, I don't think I could have sat through the rest of the movie."

"Me neither." He put his arm around her shoulders and pulled her close. She drew comfort from his touch as her trembling settled quietly to a low hum. "How about we get out of here? I'm ready for lunch."

Jeannine opened her mouth to speak, but she was interrupted by the museum manager. "Oh, wait, you two. I'd like to thank you for your efforts," he said, and handed several museum passes to them. "I know it's not much, considering the effort you two made just now, but please come back and see us again." He smiled, anxiety showing in his features. "Maybe you can finish watching the film another time."

"I'd like that, thank you," Jeannine said.

"Me, too." Miklo removed his hand from Jeannine's shoulder and shook hands with the manager. "I'm sure we'll be back."

"How about for the Chocolate Fantasy Ball? That's in a week or so, and I would be delighted to give you complimentary tickets. Can't buy them any more. We've sold out completely but I've got a couple left in my office. I'd be happy to send them to you."

"Aren't these tickets very expensive?" Jeannine asked, hesitating as she bit her lower lip. "I'm not sure that would be appropriate for us to accept." Though she wanted to go, she wouldn't rope Miklo into a date like that. He would feel obligated to take her, and she didn't need that in her life.

"Nonsense. Your community service today has more than earned you the right to have dinner and chocolate at our expense. Besides, if you come, it would provide some invaluable publicity for the museum." He looked from Miklo to Jeannine. "Please. We need all the good publicity we can get."

Jeannine looked at Miklo, his brown eyes warm and

mysterious as he looked down at her. "Do you think it will be okay? I mean—"

"I'm sure it will be fine. If it will make you feel better, I'll check it out at the hospital. But I'm sure it will be fine. Might even give the hospital some free publicity, too."

"I'd feel better if you did." It would at least give him a way out if he didn't want to go, and she could fade into the woodwork as she usually did.

Miklo gave the museum manager the address. They left the museum and stepped into the bright sunlight of a marvelous spring day in Albuquerque. "This has turned into quite an unusual day, hasn't it? Full of…surprises."

Jeannine had to agree. As he looked at her, she was certain he meant more than the medical emergency. "Let's get some food. I'm starving after all that." Now she wasn't sure whether the trembling in her limbs was from the exertion or Miklo's close proximity and the casual way he touched her without seeming aware of it.

"The restaurant I had in mind isn't that far. Want to walk?" he asked as he put on sunglasses.

"Yes. I worked up a good sweat in there." She needed the fresh air to shake off the feelings she was starting to have for Miklo, as well as needing the stress relief after the incident. But as they walked, Miklo took her hand again and the tension between her shoulders evaporated as if it had never been. Why was Miklo having such an effect on her? Her ex-fiancé had never made her tremble with a touch. Was her reaction to

Miklo just a case of being affection starved or did it run deeper than that? Despite having sworn off men entirely, had she found one that could actually be as caring and loyal as he appeared to be?

Minutes later they found an outside table at a lovely Mexican restaurant. "If you're too warm, why don't you take your sweatshirt off?" Miklo suggested and removed his to reveal a skin-tight T-shirt that outlined every muscle in his arms and chest.

Jeannine swallowed and choked down the gasp of appreciation the sight inspired and took a quick drink from her water glass.

Oh, my.

The waiter interrupted. "Hello. What can I get you to drink?"

They ordered, and Jeannine hoped that Miklo would be distracted by a change in conversation topic.

"May I see your wrist?" he asked, and held out his hand across the table.

"What?" She blinked several times, hoping she had heard him incorrectly, and kept her hands clenched in her lap.

"Last evening I couldn't see the scar on your wrist very well, and I'd like to take a look at it again." Wiggling his fingers, he motioned for her arm.

Resisting didn't seem like the right thing to do. But, then, neither did displaying her scar for him to see in the bright light of day.

"I know you're uncomfortable, but you have to show someone sometime, don't you?"

"Well, no, not really. I can just go around covered up the rest of my life."

"And hide that beautiful figure of yours? Beauty should be enjoyed and shared, not hidden away."

"Oh, I'm no beauty." Terrence had made sure she'd known that. Time after time he'd compared her to other women who were truly beautiful. Now, with the scars on her body, she'd never be considered beautiful.

"Jeannine," he said, his gaze intent on hers as he leaned forward. "I have traveled to the most exotic lands in the world and have seen many beautiful women." Reaching under the table, he gently grasped her hand in his and raised it. "Beauty is not just an issue of skin and good bone structure. It's an unknown quality that a woman portrays that draws a man's eye." Drawing light circles in her palm with the tip of his finger, he continued. "Confidence, intelligence, spontaneity, caring, and humor are on the top of my list of attractive attributes and you've got all of them." Miklo rubbed his thumb on the inside of her hand. "You're more of a beauty than you know."

"I'm covered in scars, Miklo," she whispered, tears pricking her eyes. "I'm hideous. And I don't know if I'll be able to have children of my own. So I'm certainly more flawed than you'd like to believe."

"Who says perfection is interesting?" Miklo shrugged and drank from his water glass. "In my book, perfection is overrated." He sighed. "But I'm sorry about the fertility question. Are you certain?"

"No. They saved one ovary and tube, the uterus is

okay, too, but with the amount of infection I had, there's no telling how things will work if I get to that point."

"Do you want to have children?" he asked, his eyes now guarded.

"I don't know. I grew up thinking I'd have a family some day. Don't all little girls?" She huffed out a trembling breath as every fear she'd ever known churned away in her stomach. "I think the time for that dream has come and gone already." Facing that fact was a hard reality, but she'd have to accept it sooner or later.

"There are so many breakthroughs in fertility medicine these days, there's no telling what could—"

"No." Jeannine pressed a hand to her forehead, trying to suppress the ache forming there. "Can we talk about something else for a while?"

"Sure."

Their lunches arrived and they ate in silence for a moment. "I'm sorry if I've upset you," he said. "I never meant to hurt or offend you."

"It's okay, Miklo. It's something I've got to get used to, haven't I?" she asked and avoided his gaze.

Miklo put down his fork and waited for her to look up. "Do you trust me?" he asked. Startled, she didn't speak. After a moment she nodded. "Let me see your arm." This time, she placed her hand in his without hesitation.

Looking down at her wrist, he now saw in the bright light the scar that would never go away. "This is deep," he admitted, and turned her wrist to see it from another angle. "There are things that can be done to decrease them, there are creams and, as a last resort, surgery, if you'd like to go that far." Running one thumb over the mark, he held onto her. "You won't be perfect, but pretty close. You have beautiful skin."

"Miklo, I just agreed that I trusted you. Don't go lying to me now," she said, and removed her hand from his and picked up her fork.

"We all have scars, Jeannine. Some are just more visible than others." With a sigh he took a few bites of his meal, then gave up any pretense of interest in it. "Since you shared some of your past with me, I'll share some of mine with you." That was only fair, right? And he had just asked her to trust him. The best way to earn her trust was to give her his. "A few years ago my wife died in a car accident. She was six months pregnant, and I lost the baby, too."

"Oh, my God, Miklo. I'm so sorry," she said in a sharp whisper. The compassion in her voice was almost his undoing. "I had no idea. I'm sitting here whining about my problems when you've lost so much."

"I was supposed to take Darlene to a baby shower for my cousin, but I was working, and she went alone." Memories of that night would haunt him always. "It was monsoon season, and the roads were wet everywhere. Another car lost control and hit her head on."

"A car accident isn't your fault," she said. "You can't believe that."

"I believe that I wasn't where I should have been. If I had just taken a few hours off, I could have saved them. I know it."

"Just how much power do you think you have, Dr. Kyriakides?" she asked, challenge in her eyes.

"None at all." That had been made abundantly clear to him.

"Playing the 'what-if' game will only drive you mad, you know that, don't you?" she asked. "I had six months to play it myself recently and it didn't accomplish a damned thing."

"You're right. In my head I know you're right. But I just can't let it go yet." He gave an awkward smile. "I didn't mean to put a damper on our day, but I wanted you to know this about me."

Reaching out, she squeezed his hand with hers. "Thank you for telling me. Seems like we're two of a kind, aren't we?"

"We are."

Conversation drifted to more comfortable topics, and Miklo didn't press Jeannine any further on the scar issue. He had enough of his own scars to deal with, so he could hardly cast any stones for covering hers.

"Obviously, with such language skills, you'll have traveled a great deal, right?"

"Yes. Greece, of course, Spain, and Italy are my favorite places to visit." Sipping his iced tea, he studied her. "Your eyes remind me of the Aegean Sea. Not quite blue, not quite green, but definitely crystal clear and fathomless."

"You're going to make me blush." And, in fact, she did flush, the heat rising in her neck and face.

"I'm sorry. I didn't mean to embarrass you, but what

I said is still true." He left money on the table for the bill and stood.

"It's okay." Jeannine stood, and he pulled her chair out. They walked several blocks through the adobe structures of Old Town, decorated with items of native American and Spanish influence. *Ristras*, dried red chili peppers strung together in vertical bundles, hung from almost every door or window, creating bright spots of color in an otherwise earth-tone shopping district.

"Jeannine?"

She jumped, realizing she had been in her own world for a few moments. "Sorry. What?"

"I asked if you were ready to go home or if you wanted to do something else."

"Oh, yes. I didn't mean to keep you. I'll go home. It's been quite a day." And she didn't want to take over his entire day off. With three brothers, he probably had family events to attend.

"I just want to call and check on Roberto before we head back." Reaching into a pocket, he pulled out his cellphone.

Amusement swirled in her eyes, and Miklo paused. "What?"

"We can never quite let it go, can we?" She indicated the phone in his hand. "The job, I mean. Even with all of the other things going on in our lives, we just can't stop being a nurse or a doctor any time we want to. Leaving work at work just doesn't happen for us. It's in our blood, isn't it?"

Impressed by her understanding, Miklo nodded,

wishing his wife had seen things that way. She hadn't been in the medical field and her insight had lain in other areas. The past was the past and it needed to stay where it was. But it rode his back wherever he went and his efforts to move on had failed. "You're right. Sometimes I wish I could just step away from it, maybe into something like dermatology. But unless I'm out of the country, I feel like I'm on duty all the time."

"Well, if we go to the Chocolate Fantasy Ball, you can take the night off and enjoy yourself, can't you?"

"I certainly will, but what do you mean, 'if we go,'?" He stepped closer to her, and she tilted her head back to look up at him. "You're going to go with me, dance with me, eat the most divine chocolate on the planet, and enjoy yourself, too." There was no way he was going to let her out of this.

"Isn't there someone else you'd like to take? Don't feel obliged to take me if you have other…commitments."

"There are no other commitments." Without protest, she allowed him to take her hands in his. Her touch aroused him. The desire he felt for her excited and puzzled him, but he didn't want it to go away. Activity bustled around them a few streets away. The sounds faded from his mind until they were the only two people standing there. The secrets in her eyes pulled at him, and he stepped close to her.

The afternoon sun warmed his back. Jeannine's warmth filled his arms and heated the front of him more than he had thought possible. "Jeannine," he said as he leaned closer to her. Instinct or curiosity made her lift her face to his. "You are going with me." The hesitant desire swirling in her eyes was all he needed to push him over the edge. Anticipation of tasting her again made his mouth water, and he closed the gap between them.

At first neither of them moved when he pressed his lips to hers. The shock of electricity paralyzed them momentarily. Then as her arms lifted and urged him closer, hunger overcame him, and he pulled her tightly into his arms. One hand pressed her hips against him and the other captured the back of her head. The warmth of her mouth, the heat of her tongue scorched him, imprinting the taste and feel of her on him forever. A wave of pure, unadulterated lust washed over him, hardened his body as he pressed his hips against hers. His heart rattled in his chest and the ice that had held it captive for the last three years shattered.

Jeannine slowly pulled back, but her arms remained locked around his neck and her breath came in soft gasps against his skin. Shocked surprise widened her eyes. "Oh, my," she whispered, and licked her swollen lips.

Miklo pushed her hair back from her face, then hugged her to him. "Oh, my, is right. You have no idea how good that felt."

"Actually, I have a pretty good idea myself."

Jeannine laughed, and the sound warmed him. He needed to hear the sound in his head and in his heart again, to live in it and allow it to dwell within him again.

Miklo squeezed her once more and then tucked her against his side as they returned to his car. "I'll take you home, and then go check on Roberto." Though reluctant to leave her company, he knew he had to. This unexpected attraction was happening so quickly, he was a little off-kilter. He needed a little time to think, to figure out how to feel about it. To decide if he should pursue it or walk away.

"My car is at the hospital, so you can drop me off there."

"Right," he said, his thoughts skipping ahead. "It's been such a strange day, I'd forgotten that I kidnapped you from the hospital just this morning." Weird, how time had a way of stopping at the most unexpected of times.

"Will you call me if there's any change in his condition?" she asked as they walked back to his car at the museum.

"I will." He pulled out his phone again. "Give me your number," he said, and entered it right into the phone as she recited it for him. "I'm sure he's going to be fine. Might have a few bumps in the road, but he's a really strong and healthy kid."

"He just looks so fragile covered in bandages."

"I know. They all do."

After checking in with the intensivist on duty, Miklo drove to his house. The Spanish Mediterranean style house had been a place he had once loved, bringing a sense of the ocean into the desert. Once filled with laughter and joy when it had held the promise of a family, now it was just a really big place in which to sleep and eat.

A hot shower and an omelet satisfied some of his baser needs, but a lingering restlessness prevented him from settling down for the night. Sitting home on a Saturday night wasn't his idea of a good time, but it had somehow become his norm. Weekends were for family. Since he was no longer a husband and almost a father, weekends had become torturous for him. His three brothers tried to include him, but there were times he couldn't face the love and understanding of his family. No one blamed him for not being there when Darlene had been killed. The Greek culture seemed to have a built-in understanding of tragedy.

The phone rang, pulling him from his maudlin thoughts.

"Hello?"

Rapid Spanish flowed into his ear, instantly setting him on alert. After a short, tense conversation, he knew he had to go. His help was urgently needed. When his friends called, no matter what the problem, he did what he could to help them. They would do the same for him if he needed it. The loyalty of his friends and family meant everything to him.

After a second's hesitation, he rang Jeannine.

"Hello?"

"Jeannine, it's Miklo. I need your help. Are you willing to stretch your nursing boundaries once more after such a short time?" He clutched the phone tightly. Did he have any right to ask such a thing of her? Though he knew an abundance of medical people, Jeannine was the first one he thought of for this situation.

"What's wrong? Is it Roberto again?" Concern emanated from her voice.

"No. A friend called from Las Cruces. He runs a small hospital down by the Mexican border, and he's got a kid in serious trouble. Major trauma."

"I'm assuming if he's calling you to come there, the patient is too fragile to transport?"

"Yes. We can be there in an hour by plane." Again, he hesitated. Was he just being selfish to want her with him, or was she truly the right person for the job? If she declined, he would know he'd been wrong to ask. Why he wanted her with him remained a mystery to him. Perhaps spending time with her would clear that away.

"Plane?" she squeaked. "As in the small plane you mentioned earlier today?"

"Yes. I promise you'll be perfectly safe in it. I'm a licensed pilot and have flown safely for years." The plane that he now owned had once been his saving grace.

"I'll come. What do I need to do?" she asked, her voice shaky.

After a slight pause the sound of her voice in his ear made him more resolved than ever to keep that promise. "Pack a bag for a couple of days. We'll likely be back tomorrow evening, but just in case we aren't, bring a few things. Can you be ready in forty-five minutes?"

"Yes."

CHAPTER NINE

JEANNINE tried not to put too many claw marks in the control panel of Miklo's plane. Hyperventilating wasn't a very good idea, but she seemed incapable of breathing at a normal rate. "Try cupping your hands around your mouth and slow your breathing." Miklo's voice crackled through the headset into her ears. "Otherwise you're going to vomit."

"Oh, great. Yet another way to humiliate myself in front of you." Taking his advice, Jeannine cupped her hands around her mouth and forced her breathing to slow. "You really know how to show a girl a good time, Miklo."

"We're almost there. If you can hang on for twenty minutes, we'll be through the roughest part." He glanced at her. "I'm sorry. The weather doesn't always cooperate."

"Welcome to life in New Mexico, right?" Nodding, Jeannine managed to swallow down her nerves. "Talk to me," she said as her stomach pitched with the rough movement of the plane. "Distract me somehow. When did you start flying?"

Miklo paused for a second, then began to speak. "I

learned to fly about ten years ago. Driving places just took too long for me, and I needed the peace that flying alone gave me."

The sound of his voice soothed her nerves, calmed her fears, and she could breathe again. "Does flying help with job stress?"

"Somewhat. No pagers. No cellphones. Nothing except me and the wind." He paused a moment and gave a deep sigh. "After Darlene was killed I flew a lot. Just being up here helped keep me away from everything that waited for me down there."

Jeannine spoke into the headset. "Go on."

"It wasn't like I wasn't dealing with the pain. But once in a while I just needed a break from it." The breaks had helped. Helped him realize that although he hadn't loved his wife as deeply as he had wanted, he had loved their life together and their plans to create a family together. They had been friends for many years and had respected each other. Theirs had been a match based on friendship and loyalty and love of family.

"Coming from such a large family, I'm sure they've been a comfort to you."

"Yes, but…I feel foolish confessing this to you. But it seems sometimes that *they* are ready for me to move on, find a new wife, and get busy making babies again." He sighed. "I know they mean well, but I just can't take that step yet. Maybe not ever." The thought of creating a new family wasn't what scared him. It was the thought of losing them that chilled him.

"I'm sure they mean well, but that is a difficult situation to think about. When you love someone a great deal, it's difficult to let them go and live life without them."

"Sounds like you've have some experience there, too."

"Oh, I've had my heart broken a few times, but nothing like what you've lost." The loss of a few boyfriends over the years was nothing compared to what he'd gone through. "Terrence, my ex-fiancé, hurt me the worst, but now I'm realizing that he wasn't right for me." So not right, it wasn't funny. How had she not realized that sooner? Had she just been so lonely and starved for affection that she had accepted anyone?

"How long had you been together before the pregnancy?" he asked.

"Two years." Two very long, very unproductive years.

"I'm sorry, Jeannine. Truly sorry about the baby." Yet another shared tragedy between them.

"Me, too. Who knows? Maybe some day I'll be able to have a child." She shrugged and sat upright, then looked at him, the green lights from the control panel eerily illuminated her face. "I wasn't pregnant for very long before my tube ruptured. Then I was so sick I didn't really have a chance to think about anything except living through the experience." She returned to her previous position with her hands cupped around her mouth.

Moments passed in silence as Miklo concentrated on flying. "It's a glorious sight, flying into the city at night, isn't it?"

"Seeing it would mean I'd have to open my eyes."

"That would help," he said. "If you can keep your eyes on the horizon, your focus won't change all the time, and your symptoms will settle down."

Just as she opened her eyes slightly, the plane hit another air pocket, and she grabbed the control panel again. "I think I'll wait!"

Miklo chuckled and patted her leg. "We'll land in a minute and you'll be fine."

Fifteen minutes later they were on the ground, met by an emergency transport crew, and whisked away to the hospital. When they entered the hospital, Miklo pulled out his phone. "We're here," he said. After a quick conversation, he hung up. "We're going straight into the OR," he said as he escorted her down the hall. His hand on her back offered her some comfort. "Are you okay with that?"

"Fine."

Miklo stopped and turned her to face him, his dark gaze roaming over her face. "Wait a minute. When a woman answers 'fine', things usually are far from it."

Jeannine gave a small smile, knowing exactly what he meant. "It's really okay. I'm just anxious about what we're going to find when we get in there."

"Me, too." They proceeded along the dimly lit corridor toward the back of the hospital. "We'll do what we can and leave the rest to God."

Jeannine entered the women's locker room to change and returned quickly to the scrub area. She glanced at the clock as she entered the small OR. Midnight. Nearly eighteen hours had passed since she'd woken up that morning. So many things had happened in that short amount of time, so many things about herself had been forever changed.

And the night wasn't over yet.

Sensing his presence before she turned, Jeannine knew Miklo would be there. His calming energy soothed her frazzled nerves, and she huffed out a breath that chased away any lingering distractions. Even though she and Miklo were in a very foreign environment, somehow they were going to get through this together. For the sake of an injured child, they had to.

"Jeannine, this is my friend, José Martinez. He's the surgeon who called me." The men were close in coloring, beautiful, golden Latin skin, dark eyes and the blackest of hair. But Miklo's features called to her, whereas José looked just like a very attractive man. There was no heightening of her pulse as there was when she looked at Miklo.

"Thank you so much for coming," José said in a raspy voice that somehow suited him. "Your assistance means much to me. Not everyone would drop what they were doing to help a stranger."

"I'm happy that Miklo invited me to come along." Jeannine shook his warm hand.

"Gracias." The three moved into the OR and the real work began. "The boy was struck by a speeding truck and dragged for half a mile. He has had one surgery to fix his internal injuries, which has been successful. Unfortunately, the injuries to his face are so extensive

that I would trust no one except Miklo to operate on him."

"Thank you, my friend." Miklo acknowledged the compliment. "You would do the same for me."

The confidence shared between the two friends boosted her flagging esteem and the fatigue that crawled along her skin evaporated. A little trust went a long way, and she trusted Miklo's skills as a surgeon. More importantly, she was beginning to trust Miklo as she had trusted no man. Every moment she spent with him solidified that trust even more.

"Ready when you are, Doctors."

Five hours later, the surgery ended with Miklo more frustrated than he'd been in years. He was so helpless. So powerless against the devastation of such injuries. Pins, and screws, and more than a few curses were what held the boy's face together. "I'm afraid that is all we will be able to do for him for now," José said as he removed his OR attire with a heavy sigh, appearing as affected as Miklo. "I'll take you to the guest quarters, and you can get some rest. It has been a long day for us all."

"There should be more we can do. If he is stable enough we can transfer him to the University Hospital in Albuquerque." Miklo ran a hand through his hair, trying to think of anything that would change the situation to one he could deal with. "People—*children*—shouldn't have to suffer like this," Miklo said as a knot of anger formed in his jaw.

"No, they shouldn't, but they do, and we must accept

it," José said, the look in his eyes sad. "His family is very poor and would not be able to make the trip. First we see how he does before we take him from his home and the people that love him."

"You're right," Miklo said and nodded, his eyes downcast but his frustration still obvious. "You're right." Every part of him that was a healer wanted to argue, wanted to rage at the injustice against an innocent child, but he knew he didn't have the power to change it. As a surgeon he only had so much control, and he wasn't deluded enough to think otherwise.

"When we went into the OR you said we would do what we could," Jeannine said in a gentle tone, reminding him of his own philosophy. She touched him on the arm, and he faced her, searching for something in her face. Some reason to make all of this effort worth the cost to everyone.

Reaching out to her, Miklo pulled the hair cover away and let her hair spill over her shoulders. "You're right, too. There is only so much we can do, the rest is out of our hands. Sometimes I don't know when to let go."

"Let me take you to your quarters," José said, and led them from the OR. "Your bags should be there already." The men spoke a few moments in Spanish, and then they arrived at the bungalow, just a hundred yards from the hospital.

"This is lovely," Jeannine said, taking in the little cottage with its furnishings in the style of Old Mexico.

"The refrigerator is full of food, and there is excellent tequila in the cupboard. Help yourselves to whatever you need," José said, and stifled a yawn. "I will come get you at noon."

Jeannine entered the bungalow and stretched, stifling a yawn.

"Why don't you have a shower first? I'll see what's available for food," Miklo suggested, knowing he wouldn't be able to go to sleep right away. Reviewing the operation was one way of deciding whether his efforts had been good enough.

"Sounds good." Jeannine found her overnight bag in one bedroom, gathered the necessary items and disappeared into the bathroom.

Miklo opened the heavy draperies in the living area. The windows faced the city and offered a picturesque view. The pre-dawn light of the very early morning cast a soft peach glow onto the landscape surrounding the desert city. The tension in his shoulders eased a notch as he turned away from the sight to rummage around in the refrigerator. Fresh fruit, tortillas, and a pitcher of citrus juice sat inside. He took the items out and arranged them on the table. He hoped Jeannine liked… When he realized what he was doing, he stopped.

Fixing a meal, seeing to the comfort of another person, was almost…domestic. Something he hadn't realized he'd missed. Reaching for the tequila, he added a splash and some ice cubes to the juice for a mild margarita. He didn't need it to fall asleep, but just a taste would offer him some comfort.

"This looks fabulous," Jeannine said as she walked barefoot across the tiled floor.

She had changed into casual clothing rather than sleeping garments and appeared refreshed after a shower. Her long wet hair was combed back from her face, revealing eyes that sparkled when she looked at him, and his throat tightened.

She was beautiful.

Something stirred within him that he hadn't acknowledged for a long time. Now that his feelings were waking again, he wasn't sure that this was a good idea, being alone with her in such intimate surroundings. "Tired?"

"Not a bit. I'm wide awake now. And starved." She reached for a piece of fruit. "Everything is so beautiful, thank you."

Miklo swallowed and stepped back a pace from her. The clean fragrance of a simple soap washed over him, and he shoved his hands into his pockets to keep from reaching out to her. "My turn. Help yourself." Not bothering with a razor, he showered, changed, and returned to find Jeannine in a comfortable chair facing the windows and the sunrise. A plate of fruit and a half-full glass of juice sat on the table next to her.

And she was sound asleep. Looking down at her, he took the chance to examine her without making her uncomfortable. She was a beautiful woman. Long limbed, long hair the color of melted caramel, lush breasts that rose and fell with her gentle breathing. All of the physical attributes were certainly there, but it was the sparkle of amusement in her eyes, the tremor of laughter in her voice, and her personal strength that intrigued him more than anything else. Her scars were irrelevant. Exotic women were a dime a dozen in his world. One with a gentle heart was a rare find.

This rare find was about to slide out of her chair onto the floor. With one arm behind her knees and one behind her shoulders, he picked her up.

Startled, she clamped her arms around his neck. "What?" she said, her eyes wide, but still filled with sleep.

"Nothing," he said as he maneuvered through the cottage. "You fell asleep in your chair."

"I did not."

Miklo laughed. "Yes, you did. I heard you snoring."

Jeannine gasped. "Miklo Kyriakides, I do *not* snore." She wiggled her feet. "Put me down before you have a hernia. I'm too big."

"You're not heavy, just tall. Very tall." They neared the bed, and he released her legs, allowing her to slide against his body.

That was his first mistake.

Torturing himself with her hadn't been his intention, but now he had no intention of letting her go without tasting her lips again.

"Miklo," she whispered, and her gaze dropped to his mouth. "I'm not...prepared for anything...between us." But her rapid breathing that echoed his own told him she was not unaffected by his closeness.

"Neither am I." He pushed her damp hair back from

her face. "But there's something going on between us that will need further exploration." His hand drifted downward to rest on her hip, slowly drawing her against him. That was his second mistake, but one he seemed powerless to resist.

"I see."

Her cautious gaze lifted, and the desire swirling in her eyes only fueled his want of her. He shouldn't. He ought not. But he wanted her anyway. Wanted her in a way he hadn't wanted a woman in so very long. "I'm exhausted, and so are you. We both need some rest, but I…want to hold you while we sleep." Nuzzling her soft cheek against his made him think of things he shouldn't, made him want things he couldn't have, but he'd be damned if he'd give up this time out of time, this moment that had come out of nowhere, without drawing some of it inside himself to savor later. Was it so wrong? "It's been a long time since I've wanted…this," he whispered, his voice tight with emotion.

Jeannine turned her face toward him, her light breath fanning his skin. "Me, too." Cupping his cheek with her hand, she looked deep into his eyes, searching for answers he didn't know if he had.

She pulled his head down and kissed him.

He groaned as an unexpected flood of sexual energy surged through him. Although minutes ago he'd said he wasn't prepared, in seconds his body was indeed more than ready to lead the charge out of celibacy.

Lowering her to the bed, he pressed his weight on top of her, and devoured her mouth. Years of frustration and loneliness melted away as Jeannine wrapped her arms around him and held him tight. Whatever was wrong with him was healing right now in Jeannine's arms. Each breath he took filled his senses with her. Her soft breasts pressed into his chest, the flare of her hips drew his hand. Each gasp, each moan, seared his mind and body with his need of her.

The weight of him pressed down on her felt more right than anything had in a long time. Kissing him, touching him, holding him against her was the stuff fantasies were made of. He stirred her, he thrilled her, and if she wasn't careful, she was going to fall hard for this man. So much of her life had been filled with doing the right thing for the wrong reasons. Now she just wanted to be free to do what she wanted, what she needed, and now she needed Miklo. Bending one knee, she hooked her foot around his leg and held on.

Pressing a row of kisses along the soft column of her neck, Miklo halted at the collar of her shirt and raised his head with a groan of frustration. "If I don't stop now, I'm not going to be able to," he said, his voice a husky whisper. "Whatever is going on between us is too easy, too enticing, for me to resist much longer." Every inch of him trembled with unexpected need.

"I'm sorry. I didn't meant to…" She tried to pull away, but he held her fast.

"Shh. Don't be sorry." His hungry gaze raked over her rumpled clothing. "I'm not. I want this as much as you do. I can see it in your eyes, feel it in your kiss. You just don't know how tempting you are to me. But I don't want to rush into something neither of us is prepared for." He kissed her swollen lips gently and moved his weight off her, then gathered her back against his chest and settled onto the pillows. "Will you lie here with me and sleep?" he asked. "I'll understand if you don't want to, if I've scared you."

"No, I want to stay," she whispered, and settled back against his chest. More than you'll ever know, she thought. The first man not disgusted by her disfigurement was one who had his own issues, deep scars, that hurt him on the inside more than hers did on the outside.

If all she ever had with him was this one moment in time, she was going to take it. She knew he wanted her, she felt the burning heat of his arousal straining against her backside. Some deep-seated feminine part of her personality found great satisfaction in his swift reaction. Miklo, a man who moved heaven and earth for others, who flew an airplane through desert storms to come to the aid of an injured child, was quickly becoming entirely too hard to resist.

If things had been different between them, if they had each been in different places in their lives, they might not have let go of each other tonight. But here and now their lives were too far apart to indulge in a selfish sexual tryst that would leave them both empty inside.

The deep rhythmic movement of his chest told her that he had succumbed to sleep. Content to rest in his arms as long as possible, she was determined to savor every second with Miklo strong and warm beside her.

CHAPTER TEN

STARTLED, heart racing, Miklo opened his eyes and tried to remember where he was. As memories of the last day slid into his awareness, he relaxed. Midmorning arrived with blades of sunlight slicing through the window. Miklo and Jeannine lay entwined, as if they had been lovers in fact. Jeannine was still soundly asleep. She had turned toward him some time during the night, and her hand lay soft on his chest. He hadn't wakened this way since before Darlene had died. Morning cuddles and slow awakenings were something he'd missed.

Waking with a woman in his arms again was a bitter-sweet experience. He'd never expected to care for someone again, and now he didn't know what to think or what to feel. He'd pushed his feelings down so far he didn't know how to call them back again.

Was it the forced intimacy he and Jeannine had shared over the last few days that created the illusion of caring? Or had he somehow managed to allow her into his heart without even knowing, without being aware of her entrance?

As he closed his eyes, images of his wife fluttered through his mind. Memories of the life they had shared no longer wielded the sharp edges they once had. He no longer bled at the mere thought of her. Perhaps he was healing and the time had finally come to move on. With a sigh, he cuddled Jeannine closer. The ticking clock in his head stopped, and he was able to sleep again without dreams.

Sunlight streaming through the window roused Jeannine. As soon as she moved, Miklo awoke. "What's wrong?" hc said, and blinked several times.

"Nothing. Just waking up," Jeannine said, easing from his warm embrace. "I'm going to get some juice—want some?"

"Sure."

After a light breakfast, they returned to the hospital to check on their patient.

"He's holding his own, thanks to you both," José said. "I'm so impressed that you were able to come immediately. You certainly saved his life."

"That's one of the benefits of having your own plane," Miklo said.

"Should there be anything I can do for you, please let me know. I will come at once," José said.

Miklo gave Jeannine a sideways glance, but spoke in Spanish to José.

José grinned and looked at Jeannine.

She crossed her arms and narrowed her eyes. "Hey,

now. What are you two talking about? That's not fair since I don't understand Spanish."

Miklo grinned. "It's a surprise." He took a set of keys from José and waved once, then led Jeannine out of the hospital.

"Where are we going? I'm not sure if I can trust you any more, Miklo," she said with a laugh. Heat pulsed in her chest, warming her, knowing that whatever was going on was going on just for her.

Miklo laughed. "You know you can trust me. It's just a little side trip I want to take you on before we go back to Albuquerque."

"What is it?"

"We're going for a drive." He led her to a well-worn Jeep.

Jeannine climbed into the open vehicle. There was no top, nothing except a roll-bar between her and all the fresh air she could want. "Where are we going?"

Miklo got in and started the cranky engine. "Juarez."

"That's in Mexico… I don't have my passport."

"It *is* Mexico, and you don't need it." Miklo put the Jeep into gear, and they took off.

"I've always heard they're dangerous places, border towns."

"Not with me around it isn't. I speak the language, and we're only going to be there for a couple of hours, then we'll head back to reality." He considered her seriously for a moment. "Since we were so close to the border, and you said you'd never been out of the country, I thought this might be an opportunity to try it."

Jeannine swallowed down the spasm of fear that tried to intrude. Since she'd met Miklo, she'd done so many things outside of her comfort zone that she didn't know where that zone began or ended any more. Fear no longer seemed like something to be…afraid of. "Let's go."

"Great. It's about an hour's drive, so you can relax and take in the scenery while I play tour-guide."

An hour later, after securing a parking spot and paying a teenager an outrageous amount to watch the vehicle, Miklo and Jeannine walked across the causeway into the city of Ciudad Juarez, Mexico.

The sights, the sounds, the smells all melded together into a symphony of sensation that was all new and exciting to her. Jeannine tried to take everything in at once as they strolled along the walkway of the open-air marketplace.

"You look like a *turista*," Miklo said with a grin.

"Well, I am."

"Let's keep going," he said, and took Jeannine's hand.

"Going where? This is an interesting place. Why don't we stop here?" she asked with a frown, but allowed him to direct their path.

"There's another marketplace farther along that caters more to the locals. This is just for unsuspecting tourists."

"Oh. I wouldn't have known that."

"Then it's good you are taking your first excursion out of the country with someone who does, right?"

"Right."

After an hour or two spent in the marketplace, another span of time spent lingering over a Mexican dinner on the open patio of an unnamed restaurant, and exotically rich coffee, their day was almost over.

With each passing moment, Jeannine felt herself slide down the slope she had cautiously guarded against. But she knew she was falling for Miklo in a big way. Panic flared in her chest, and she tried to ease the tight feeling. Falling for Miklo was not going to be good for either of them.

Miklo carried a bag with their purchases as they walked back over the border and returned to the Jeep. "Did you enjoy yourself?" he asked.

"Oh, yes. Very much. Thank you for taking me." Spending time with him away from work, away from the city, away from everyone, was something she'd never have dreamed of. Something she would cherish.

"You're welcome."

They returned to Albuquerque, and Jeannine was grateful to land on her home turf. So much had happened, so much had changed, that she needed some time to think.

"Here you are," Miklo said as he pulled into her driveway.

"It seems like days since you picked me up, not just twenty-four hours. Time is a strange thing, isn't it?"

Miklo leaned his head back against the headrest. "It is. We sure packed a lot into a day."

"More than I think I ever could have." She paused and bit her lower lip. "Do you want to come in?"

Turning toward her, Miklo searched her eyes in the dim light from the dashboard. "I don't think I'd better right now."

"Okay. I'm sure you're going to be up early tomorrow."

He shifted in the seat and faced her fully. "It's not that."

The sound of his voice in the close confines of the car made her want to shiver. He was so intense, so male. "It's okay, Miklo. Really. You don't need a reason." God, she was so stupid sometimes.

"Jeannine," he said, and reached out to cup his hands around her cheeks. "This is why."

He kissed her. The first touch of her skin under his hands, the first burst of her fragrance washing over him, the first touch of her eager mouth beneath his, sent a shockwave of desire through him.

He shouldn't want, he didn't have the right to, but he did. He would never forgive himself for what happened to his family, but he was still a man with all the baser needs of one. Jeannine's presence brought out every one of them, and he pulled back from her. "I want you too much right now."

"I see." She curved her hair behind one ear. "That's bad, then, isn't it?"

Miklo choked out a laugh. "I don't know what it is, but every time I'm alone with you… Anyway, I just don't think we should tempt fate too far. It has a way of coming back to repay you at the worst of times."

Jeannine gathered her things and faced Miklo. "I

had a wonderful time. Except for the airplane part. Thank you."

"You're welcome."

She left the car and hurried to her house. She opened the door and with a wave disappeared inside.

Before he could change his mind, Miklo backed the car out of the driveway and drove home.

Jeannine couldn't believe how slowly the day was moving. Though it was only two p.m., she felt as if she'd been at work for twelve hours already. Her patient was stable, so she joined her colleague Trish in the staff lounge for a break. They chatted a few minutes, with Trish snapping open the pages of a fashion magazine.

"How was your weekend?" Trish asked, not looking up.

"Fine," Jeannine said. Oh, it had been more than fine, but she wanted to keep her thoughts to herself. Even though Trish looked set to become a true friend, the experiences with Miklo over the weekend were too precious to share just yet. Too unnerving to let herself think about for too long. "I was hoping I'd be assigned to Roberto today. I'd like to check on him."

"Sure. Go ahead. I'll watch your patient for a while. If anything changes, I'll page you." Trish waved a casual hand at her.

Jeannine made her way down the hall to Roberto's room. Roberto had progressed enough to be moved out of the ICU and into the general pediatric unit. When she entered his room, he sat up, his eyes bright.

"Hi, there. *Como esta usted?*" she asked him.

He spoke quickly to her and gestured to his face, which was still swollen in areas and colored purple and green but had improved dramatically. She laughed at his antics, not understanding anything he said. Jeannine asked for some interpretation from one of the nurses who spoke fluent Spanish.

"He's just excited and wanted to thank you for helping Dr. Miklo fix his face. He remembers you and how you helped him." Roberto stood on his bed and reached for Jeannine. He hugged her tightly and said, "*Gracias.* Papa say thanks to you."

"You are very welcome, Roberto." Tears pricked Jeannine's eyes at his heartfelt gesture, and she hugged his small body to her, wishing that some day she could have a child of her own but knowing it was probably impossible. She would have to content herself with taking care of other people's children in the hospital.

Roberto released Jeannine with a squeal and began talking excitedly in Spanish again. Jeannine turned and her heart gave a flip as Miklo walked into the room. Roberto talked to him, and Miklo nodded, then brought a small car from his labcoat pocket. Jeannine grinned. Without having understood the conversation, she got the idea from the eagerness on Roberto's face.

"He asked if I brought another car so that we could race," Miklo said.

The look in his eyes took away her ability to give a sensible response. The spark of interest grew as his gaze lingered on her mouth, and she resisted the urge to lick her lips. "I see you came prepared. Who do you think is going to win?"

"He will. Hands down. I'm a bad driver." He examined Roberto as they played with the cars.

Jeannine knew he assessed the boy as they played, and it seemed more like fun than a doctor's exam. She gave Miklo full credit for keeping the boy as comfortable as possible while gathering the information he needed.

"I'd better get back to the ICU. Things were slow for a while, but I don't want to be gone too long."

"I'll walk down with you," Miklo said. "I'm about to head out, anyway."

They walked in silence to the stairwell, and Miklo opened the door. Anticipation hummed through her. Lord, she wanted Miklo to touch her again, but she didn't think it wise. For either of them.

The door slammed closed, and he spun her around. She reached out for him with a glad cry. The second his lips met hers, she knew she was heading down the path of heartache, but she was powerless to run the other way.

When he lifted his head, he stepped back from her. "I told myself when I saw you again that I wasn't going to feel anything special, I wasn't going to want to touch you again, but…Jeannine, I do." He stroked a hand over her cheek. "I enjoyed our weekend."

"So did I." More than he could know. She'd relived every moment in her mind over the last few hours.

Miklo took her hand and headed down the stairs. "We'd better get out of here before I'm accused of accosting a co-worker in the stairwell," he said.

Jeannine's laughter echoed off the walls. "I don't think that will be an issue. I might just as well be accused of the same thing."

He opened the door to the PICU and dropped her hand. They returned to being just coworkers, and Jeannine was a little disappointed, though she knew it was for the best. Instead of leaving, he pulled her aside as a patient was wheeled by on a gurney. "Incidentally, I did check with Risk Management about us accepting the tickets for the ball, and they said it was just fine." He nodded. "I mentioned the part about publicity, and they thought that we could use some good publicity, as well as the museum."

"Oh, good," she said, and touched her hand to her chest. "I didn't want us to get into trouble over it."

"If it had been an issue, I would have just paid for the tickets," he said. "No problem."

Jeannine stared at him. "You really would have?"

"Absolutely. Taking you to the Chocolate Fantasy Ball would be worth more than what the tickets cost. I'll see you on Saturday. Pick you up at six?"

Jeannine nodded, unable to speak as she stared at him.

"Will you wear the dress we got in Mexico?"

"Oh, no. It's too revealing." The thought of being so exposed in a large crowd made her tremble. Revealing herself to Miklo was one thing, but to a room of strangers was quite another. "You really shouldn't have bought it."

"So wear something over it, a shawl or something." His eyes turned hungry. "I'd like to see you in it."

"Miklo…" she whispered, uncertainty crawling through her.

"You've stretched your boundaries a lot recently. What's one more?"

"I'll think about it." It was the best she could offer right now.

"Okay. See you Saturday night."

"Okay." She watched him go and wondered at the heaviness of her heart. Should she really go through with it?

"Jeannine!" Trish squealed, and motioned her into the staffroom.

Jeannine jumped, then ran inside. "What's wrong? Are you okay?"

Trish glared at Jeannine and crossed her arms. "That's what I want to know. What was all that with Dr. Hottie? *See you Saturday night?* Spill it!"

Despite a great desire not to, Jeannine flushed. "I'm not sure what you—"

"Oh, don't give me that," Trish interrupted, and hopped onto the table. "You have a date with the sexiest doctor in the entire hospital, don't you?"

"It's…it's…not really a date," she said in a rush. "It's more of a…public relations obligation." That sounded good, didn't it?

"I knew it!" Trish jumped down, took Jeannine by the arm and dragged her to the table. "Now I want all the gory details. Every single one of them."

Jeannine hesitated. "I worked with him on a complicated trauma last week, and we've been…together a few times since then."

Trish's eyes widened, and she gasped. "You mean,

as in together…together? In the buff, in a *bed* together? Oh, my God!"

"No, no, no!" Jeannine denied, and felt her flush burn her skin. "But we did actually sleep…in the same bed…together…when we were in Las Cruces. Saturday night."

"Cruces?" Trish narrowed her eyes. "I think you'd better start at the beginning. You're leaving way too many details out."

Jeannine told her story, but kept Miklo's past out of it. It wasn't her secret to share. In a way, the telling of her story was a relief, unloading all of the emotions swirling around in her. Trish sat back in her chair. "Wow. You've been through so much, and it still might not be over. There's a chance you may not conceive, isn't there?" Trish asked, and sat forward, taking Jeannine's hands in hers.

"I don't know what I was thinking, agreeing to this. But with the Chocolate Fantasy Ball coming up on Saturday night, I don't know what I'm going to do." Unexpected tears filled Jeannine's eyes. "He's going to think I'm hideous. Knowing something and seeing it in front of your face are two entirely different things."

Trish hugged Jeannine. "No, he won't. He bought you that dress and wants to see you in it, right?"

Jeannine gave a watery nod. "It fits me perfectly, except that it reveals everything I want to hide." She wiped away the tears she swore she'd never shed again. She'd stopped feeling sorry for herself a long time ago, but right now the pain of losing a baby and the uncertainty of a future one flooded over her. "I must be hormonal if I'm this weepy."

Trish brightened and gripped Jeannine's hand. "Hey! That's a good sign, then. If you think your hormonal, then you must ovulate right? That means you might be able to bear children after all." She looked at Jeannine. "I mean, that is, if you want them."

Jeannine thought a moment. Did she really want children of her own? "I haven't dared to think about it. I just don't know."

"So, what if you *could* have children with Dr. Hottie?"

"Trish! You are shameless," Jeannine cried, but then laughed and the tension in her evaporated. Trish had become a good friend. "I don't know that *Dr. Hottie* would even want to have a serious relationship with me, let alone have children with me." She smacked her friend playfully on the arm. "Let me just get through the ball without embarrassing myself."

"Okay, okay, if you insist." Trish stood and looked at the clock. "We'd better get back to work. If you want, I'll help you do your hair and make-up on Saturday night. I'm off, and it's not like I have a date or anything."

"Oh, would you really? I'd be so grateful." Jeannine grasped Trish's arm.

"I'll be there at four o'clock."

"He's not coming until six."

"Trust me," Trish said, and patted Jeannine on the

shoulder. "We're going to need every second for primping and girl time. In the meantime, you need a pair of dancing shoes and a bottle of champagne, Cinderella. You're going to need 'em both."

Jeannine nodded, thinking that they were going to need more than two hours to get her ready for the ball.

Jeannine was ready with fifteen minutes to spare. She stared at herself in the mirror. "I look like an idiot."

"You do not! Stop maligning my artistic handiwork. I'll be offended," Trish said, and circled Jeannine, adjusting a curl, the hem of her dress in the back, and then nodding her approval. "I don't know what this dress is made from, but it's lovely. Feels like silk."

"I was stupid to agree to this, good publicity or not," Jeannine said, her insides trembling. "I'll call him and cancel."

Trish moved in front of her and blocked the path to the phone. Placing her hands on her friend's face, she looked into Jeannine's eyes. "You deserve to be happy. One bad relationship doesn't mean you have to give up on ever having one." Trish lightly patted Jeannine's face. "Enjoy yourself and have a dance with Dr. Hottie for me."

Jeannine laughed. "You can't be serious for one minute, can you?"

"Sorry. Not in my job description," Trish said, and gathered her things. "I'd better get out of here before he gets here. Men aren't supposed to know about all the work that goes into such a masterpiece."

"Trish, thanks. I couldn't have faced tonight without you." She hugged her friend.

"You're gorgeous! Call me tomorrow and let me know how things went, okay?"

"Sure."

As Trish escaped out the back door, Miklo rang the front doorbell.

Oh, God. Jeannine felt like a panicked rabbit facing a deadly predator. With no other choice, she opened the door.

And almost fainted.

Oh, God. Miklo, in black tie attire, was enough to make her light-headed.

"Hi, there," he said, and smiled. He looked her up and down and whistled. "You look exquisite, Jeannine."

Oh, God! She was just going to turn into a puddle in the middle of the floor. The sound of his voice sent shivers over every inch of her skin, and she pulled the velveteen shawl closer. "Thank you. It's the dress. It would make anyone look good."

"Hardly," he scoffed, and held out his hand to her.

Tentatively, she reached out to him, knowing that if she took that step, there would be no turning back tonight. She stood on a threshold of decision in three-inch strappy sandals and a slinky black dress.

One step forward, and she closed the gap between them. "Thank you," she said.

"For what?" He tucked her hand in the crook of his elbow.

"For showing me a great time tonight."

"Better than the plane ride?"

She laughed. "Seriously, already better than the plane ride."

"You are seriously welcome. Let's go. I'm ready for my Chocolate Fantasy."

CHAPTER ELEVEN

DINNER was an absolute marvel. Multi-tiered fountains of thick, luxurious chocolate rested on tables filled with brightly colored fruits, pertly arranged crackers, and a bounty of vegetables. The fragrance of chocolate permeated the air as soon as they stepped into the ballroom, and Jeannine felt as if she had entered the inner sanctum of some secret chocolate-worshiping society.

"I didn't know so many dishes could be made using chocolate," Jeannine said as they moved along the buffet line catered by top chefs from the finest restaurants in New Mexico.

"I'm just glad there's no chocolate in the salad," Miklo said as he filled his plate.

Jeannine decided to try the chicken in chocolate sauce.

"There is chili powder and many unusual spices in it, so it's a very unique combination," the server said with a smile. "And you must try the chocolate mole for dessert."

"I will, thank you." Jeannine was glad the server offered some explanation of the food.

They found their assigned seats at a table with two other couples. "We've been here every year for the last ten years," a woman named Alessandra said. "It's always such an interesting combination of people."

They chatted with the other couples until the speaker at the front diverted their attention.

Jeannine kept the shawl tied around her shoulders and her arms tucked beneath it whenever possible. Her confidence about her scars didn't extend very far yet, and, rather than have the inquiring looks of strangers ruin her night, she kept the shawl close.

"And now I want to thank two very important people, very, very good friends of the museum." The manager who had given them the tickets stood at the front of the room.

Jeannine and Miklo faced the front as the speaker drew the attention of the entire room. As Miklo's hand drifted over her shoulder, a tremor ran through her. It was nothing she could explain, but she didn't want it to go away. This night was something she would savor the rest of her life.

"Not long ago there was a medical emergency in the museum. Fortunately for all, present were Dr. Miklo Kyriakides and his nurse, Jeannine Carlyle. With their immediate intervention, they saved the life of one of our long-time members, Mr. Carl Chase."

Applause rang through the banquet room as everyone looked around.

"Please won't you stand so these nice folks can see who you are?" the manager asked, and held a hand out toward their table.

"Miklo, what do we do?" she whispered. Having so much attention on her wasn't something she had anticipated and she tried to swallow past the lump in her throat.

He stood and pulled out her chair for her. "We accept graciously." He raised a hand and acknowledged the attention of the crowd. As everyone continued to applaud, Jeannine blushed deeply, but raised a hand, too.

"The unselfish acts you performed that day saved the life of not only one person. On a personal level you have shown me that there are still good people in the world, people who will still make sacrifices in order to help others. So from everyone at the museum, the family of Mr. Chase, and myself, thank you." He bowed to them and the crowd rose.

The orchestra waiting on the stage behind him struck up their first number.

With Miklo standing beside her, having the focus on them wasn't so bad. Some of her discomfort eased and the fluttering of her heart slowed to a more normal pace. Jeannine smiled and waved. The shawl slipped from her shoulders to puddle at her feet. Several people nearby paused and stared wide-eyed at her arms and her neck, at the scars revealed by the dress.

Jeannine froze. A sick feeling of dread turned the chocolate sauce in her stomach to mud. Miklo bent over, retrieved her shawl and deliberately placed it over the back of her chair with a meaningful glance at the others. "This will only get in the way. May I have this dance?" he asked, and without waiting for an answer took her hand, brought it to his mouth and kissed it.

Still uncomfortable with the revealing dress, she nodded and allowed Miklo to lead her to the dance floor. As she moved into his arms, the fears, the anxiety, the shame of her scars and imperfections melted away like the chocolate in the fountains. She was imperfect, she knew, but so was everyone else. Now, even in the midst of the crowd around them, there seemed to be only the two of them, with Miklo's touch warm and comforting on the bared skin at her waist.

Each circle of the dance floor brought Miklo closer to Jeannine. Something was happening to him tonight. Something he hadn't expected. But after taking her to Las Cruces, running across the border for the day, and now, holding her in his arms again, Miklo's heart beat in his chest in a way it hadn't in a very long time.

Miklo, at last, felt like a man again.

Dancing had never been like this for Jeannine. Whatever the dance, Miklo knew it and guided her around the dance floor like he'd been born to it. This was what Cinderella must have felt like at the ball, so happy, so carefree, dreading the stroke of midnight when the fantasy would all end. Each moment, each breath, each beat of her heart led her closer to the trap of falling for Miklo, but she just couldn't stop herself from walking into it.

After the first set of dancing ended, Miklo led her to the refreshment table, and she drank water to quench her thirst. Watching Miklo drink a glass of water, too, she knew her thirst for him would never end. Every time she was near him, it only became stronger, and she was sure she would find herself addicted to him, without having her need for him fulfilled.

"So, how about it? Enjoying yourself?" he asked, and stroked a hand across her cheek.

Eyes downcast, she couldn't believe he had touched her like that in such a public place in front of so many important people. As if he had actually meant it.

"Miklo, I'm having such a good time," she said, and raised her gaze to his.

"But?"

"Oh, here they are," a male voice said, interrupting their conversation. "Dr. Kyriakides? Miss Carlyle?"

They turned together to face a man in a wheelchair.

"Mr. Chase?" Miklo asked, and held out his hand. "You look much better than the last time I saw you."

"You are so right," he said, and laughed. "I wanted to thank you and your nurse for saving my life." His voice cracked and a sheen of moisture appeared in his eyes. "I have a new lease on life, thanks to you two." He reached for his wife's hand and patted it. They shared an intimate look and any lingering doubts Jeannine harbored about coming tonight vanished. This was the real reason she was here, not the publicity, not the chocolate, and not even Miklo. Well, mostly not Miklo.

Jeannine hugged the man and his wife. Seeing him in such good health after his recent near-death experience was just more proof that she was where she needed to be in her life, helping others, not worrying about her own needs and silly dreams that weren't going to go anywhere. "We were just in the right place at the right time, Mr. Chase," she said, and straightened. "Anyone would have done the same thing."

"Nonsense. You're an angel, my dear. An absolute angel," Mr. Chase said, then looked at Miklo. "I would like to do something for both of you. Please, allow me to make a donation on your behalf somewhere."

"That's not necessary, Mr. Chase," Miklo said.

"There must be some charity, someone who could use assistance that you're aware of." Mr. Chase's earnest expression tugged at Jeannine.

"Miklo," she said, and touched Miklo's arm. "What about the clinic in Cruces? Surely Dr. Martinez wouldn't refuse a charitable donation for the people there."

Miklo gave a small smile to Jeannine. "You're right." He turned back to Mr. Chase, but kept Jeannine's hand tucked into the crook of his arm. "If you're willing to donate out of the immediate community, I know of a children's clinic in desperate need of funds."

"Absolutely," Mr. Chase said, and withdrew a business card from his jacket. "Call me in a few days and give me the information. I have a few friends that could be enticed into offering their support as well."

"Excellent," Miklo said, and took the card, shook Mr. Chase's hand and watched as he wheeled away. "That was a fabulous suggestion. I should have thought of it myself," he said, and turned to face her.

"After our trip down there, it seemed a logical answer." Jeannine tried to pull away from Miklo. He was too close, too strong, too male, and her senses were being overpowered by his presence.

Looking down at her mouth, Miklo said, "Thank you." The kiss he pressed to her lips was as delicate and chaste as any she'd ever had. When he pulled away, the heat in his gaze was filled with blazing desire. "Let's get out of here."

As he drove her home, he remained silent. So many things had happened to him in the last few years. So many reasons for him to withdraw from his family, his friends, keeping work as the only source of his passion.

Now, having spent some more time with a woman so different from his wife, so different from the women in his social circle, his passion was changing. Jeannine sparked something within him that had changed him. Thanks to her, he was starting to let go of his past. As painful as it was, it finally seemed the right thing and the right time to do it. His brother had often said that he needed a new woman to forget the old one. But it hadn't been as simple as that. Darlene had been part of his life for most of his life. Leaving her memory behind wasn't easy.

Reaching out to Jeannine made him tremble. Fear and desire warred within him, and he didn't know which one was going to win.

"Miklo?" Jeannine's soft voice interrupted his thoughts. When he turned, he realized they were parked in her driveway.

"Sorry. My mind took off on me." He released his grip on the steering-wheel and dropped his hands into his lap.

"Are you okay?"

"Shall I walk you up?" he said.

"Sure." She nodded, not looking at him as she got out of the car. As she approached him she looked up. Lord, he was such a magnificent man. Proud, protective, passionate. Everything she could ever want in a man, but what could she offer him in return? She was a physically and emotionally scarred woman with a remote chance of having children. What man would want that? She bit her lip as she entered her house and sensed him walk in behind her. The darkness allowed her the freedom to speak boldly. "Did I do something wrong?" she asked, almost dreading his answer, already knowing what it would be.

"What? No," he said, and kicked the sofa. "Ow. Can you turn on the light so I can see you?"

"Do you really want to see me?" she asked in a tremulous tone, surprising herself at the boldness of her question. If she were going to make a move to change her life, the time was now.

"More than you know." His voice was a husky whisper, and she shivered as if he had touched her. Jeannine dropped her things onto the counter and turned a lamp up one notch.

"More."

Up another notch.

"More. I want to see you," he said, and moved closer to her.

Every protective instinct in her wanted her to run, but

her feet refused to move. Desire, hot in Miklo's dark, dark eyes held her motionless.

"You have done nothing wrong. It's me," he said with a sigh.

More disappointed than she could ever have imagined, she dropped her gaze as tears gathered. "Despite the best of intentions, you're still disgusted by my scars, right?" she asked.

Miklo continued moving forward until he had her backed against the wall. "Hardly. I'm less interested in your skin than how comfortable you are in it." He stroked a hand down her bare arm. "Your skin is just a wrapping, it's not what or who you are."

"Then what's wrong?" Her eyes searched his, and she cupped her hand against his cheek. Holding his gaze fast with hers, she willed him to reach out to her, to take her in his arms, to share himself with her. "Tell me what's wrong."

"It's…hard to explain, but…" He turned away and raked his hair back from his face. "Not long ago I'd have denied ever needing to feel passion again. For anyone. It was totally dead in me." Turning back to her, he caught her arm in his and pressed his mouth to the scar on the inside of her wrist. "But now you have inspired the passion in me to return. And it's a little…disturbing."

"It's only n-natural," she stuttered. "Natural to feel that way about the first person you date after…losing someone."

"Jeannine, I've dated a lot of women over the years."

The intensity in his eyes robbed her of breath. "None of them ever inspired me the way you do." He frowned and let out a sigh. "My wife and I were…comfortable with each other. Dedicated to our life together, to our families, and our friendship. What has flared between you and me is so different, so unexpected, that it has taken me by surprise."

"Miklo." Jeannine paused, searching his eyes, his face for some hint of rejection, but found nothing. The ache for him grew in her heart. She needed him right now. Gripping the lapels of his jacket in her fists, she drew him toward her. "Will you show me? The way it's supposed to be?" She tipped her face up toward his. "Please," she whispered.

"Yes." He opened his mouth over hers, swallowing down her gasp of surprise. Hot, wet, tongue searching for hers, he kissed her hard and hungrily. A thrill of desire flashed through her, and she lost herself to his touch. The intensity of him overwhelmed her.

With her back against the wall and Miklo pressed hard against her, every inch of her conformed to his body. Wrapped in his arms, Jeannine had never felt more desired than she did at that moment. She wanted it all.

Miklo didn't want to think, he just wanted to feel her silky skin against him. Keeping his lips pressed to hers, he shrugged out of his jacket and dropped it to the floor. He cupped her face in his hands, plundering her mouth with his. He'd never tasted anything as sweet as her mouth. And then he pulled back. "I want to look at you." He glanced down over the clingy black dress hugging every curve and nuance of her body. Her nipples pressed against the fabric and his mouth watered, wanting to taste every part of her. "Hold still." He started to draw the thin straps of the dress off her shoulders when her startled gasp stopped him.

"Wait. The light—"

"Don't be afraid," he said. "I'm not going to hurt you. I want to see you."

"But—"

"Shh. Shh. Let me see you. All of you." Drawing the straps off her shoulders, he moved them down, moved the dress down, and let it go.

CHAPTER TWELVE

THE dress fluttered to the floor. Very little barred his gaze from her. Her breasts stood high and proud without any bra. Pink nipples had already turned to hard peaks, rising and falling with her erratic breathing. The inward curve of her waist and softly rounded stomach made his hands itch to touch her. Black lace panties and thigh-high hose completed the ensemble, with her dress puddled around the strappy sandals.

Eyes scrunched tightly shut to hold back her tears, Jeannine turned her head to the side and waited for the door to slam behind Miklo. The sight of her had been too much for him. Her stomach quivered from holding back her breath, and she pressed one hand to her mouth.

"What are you doing?" Miklo asked, his voice surprisingly deep, surprisingly close.

"Waiting for you to leave," she whispered. Tears managed to escape and flowed down her cheeks.

"Why would I want to leave now?" Miklo pulled her hand away from her face and kissed away the moisture.

"Just look at me!" Pain in her heart was tearing her

to pieces. How could he stand there and torment her this way?

"I am. Believe me, I am." He kissed her cheek again. "Open your eyes and look at *me.*"

The smoky sound of his voice so close to her made her jump, her heart fluttering wildly. Maybe he had bad eyesight and she'd just never noticed.

"No." She almost choked on the word.

"Please?" he asked. "I want to see your eyes."

With a request like that, how could she refuse the one man who had promised to take her to paradise? Slowly, she opened her eyes and stared directly into Miklo's. Disgust, horror, guilt, and shame were remarkably absent from his eyes.

"How can you look at me like that?" Shock and surprise overcame her pain.

"Like what?" he asked, and placed his hands against the wall on either side of her, leaning ever closer.

"Like you…want me." The whisper that sprang from her came from the part of her spirit that had been trampled upon too many times.

"I do want you."

"So this is like…pity sex?" she asked, now guarded.

Miklo barked out a laugh and leaned closer, the heat coming off of him like a fire that would burn her if she got any closer. "Believe me, pity is the last thing I feel for you."

"But the scars—"

"Don't exist right now." He took one of her hands and placed it on his chest. "Inside here, mine are just as bad, though you can't see them." His gaze searched hers, and she needed to believe him. "Tonight there is nothing standing between us."

"Miklo." She breathed his name on a sigh of surrender and buried her hands in his hair.

"You are so lovely," he said, his heart racing, his breathing as fast as hers. "More than I had imagined." The fears, the guilt, the loneliness had no place between them tonight. Tonight was about feeling. Feeling her close, feeling her touch, feeling her heart beat in time with his, the rhythm of her body mirroring his. The pain that had lived in his heart eased as he looked at Jeannine standing in front of him. Wanting her was so easy, so much easier than he had imagined. All he had to do was reach out to her, and she would be his with nothing except skin separating them.

Kneeling in front of her, he pulled her closer and rubbed his face over her abdomen. He could feel the mid-line abdominal scar, but it was nothing compared to what he was feeling for her. There were other imperfections on her belly and her sides, healed puncture marks from various tubes. But they had saved her life and would forever be a reminder of her trauma. Slowly, one by one, he kissed them all, wanting to heal her, wanting to make her whole again from the inside out. He knew he couldn't do it for her as she couldn't do it for him. Perhaps together they could heal each other.

"This is so not fair," she said, her voice husky and heavy with needs he wanted to fulfill. His body had been in overdrive since they had entered her house. Now, his erection strained for release. He just hoped that he could be gentle with her and not let his own demands take over. She deserved to be pleasured.

"What's not fair?" he asked, his heart racing as he stood again.

"I'm almost naked, and you still have all your clothes on." Her bright gaze flashed over him, and his hunger for her grew.

"Not for long." Kissing her long and thoroughly, he held her tight, needing to feel her softness against him. Breathless, he pulled back and spread kisses down her neck, working his way to the notch of her collarbone. His hands spanned her waist, and he felt every rib as he stroked upward, his thumbs reaching out to stroke her nipples. "You are so delicate, I'm almost afraid to touch you."

"Please, touch me."

His mouth continued down over the curve of one breast while one hand rose to cup the other, his thumb tracing circles around a nipple. Her indrawn hiss of pleasure aroused him more than he had thought possible, and he eagerly opened his mouth over the tight peak, drawing it inside, teasing it with his tongue, savoring his first sweet taste of her.

Jeannine trembled in his arms and his body hummed in reaction. With a groan, he scooped her up in his arms. "Where is your bed?" he growled.

"End of the hall." She clasped her hands around his shoulders and pressed her face to his neck, her soft mouth spreading kisses on his skin. With long strides, he negotiated the short distance to her bedroom, stopped beside the bed and lowered her onto it.

She knelt in front of him, and her trembling fingers worked the buttons of his shirt while he fumbled with his belt. Clothing had to go—now.

Urgency pulsed through him. Ripping the shirt off, his cuff links flew across the room. He pulled her against him and dragged her down onto the bed.

"Ow," she said, and raised a hand above her head and pulled out a crunched gift bag. "What the…?"

"What is it?" he asked and took the small package from her. A note fell off it, and he picked it up. *You're going to need these. Don't forget the champagne!*

Jeannine opened one side of the decorative paper and several small items fell out. She pressed a hand to her face and stifled a groan as Miklo picked up five foil-wrapped packages that were unmistakable. "Oh, my God, Trish left this. At least there's nothing that glows in the dark."

"Wow, five. She thinks highly of me." Miklo laughed and tucked the items under a pillow. "She's right, though. We are going to need them. Champagne would add a nice touch, too." He opened a piece of chocolate. "Let's share everything." He placed the candy between his front teeth and lowered his mouth to hers. Biting the sweet against her lips, he gave her half. She chewed and swallowed, Miklo did the same.

Raising her face to him, the scent of chocolate was strong on his breath as she opened her mouth for his kiss, and thoughts of champagne fled. The glide of his tongue against hers spread fires within her. The taste of chocolate filled her senses. She thought she'd already had her chocolate fantasy tonight, but it was nothing compared to this. Holding himself above her, he pressed his lips into hers. A deep ache within her expanded until she was a throbbing mass of churning need. "Miklo." Her whisper was lost in the deep of the night.

Her breasts tingled for his touch again and moisture pooled between her legs. Her female flesh throbbed with an ache she knew only he could satisfy.

His urgent hands stripped her remaining clothing and shoes away. As she looked at the desire in his eyes she knew he saw *her*, wanted *her*, needed *her*. Nothing else mattered and the scars began to fade.

Reaching out to him, she shoved his clothing off. "Show me. Show me now." The heat of his arousal straining against her leg made her gasp.

Before she could reach out to him, he pulled a nipple into his mouth and pressed his fingers into her moist folds. Ecstasy filled her, and she arched her back, pressing more fully into his hand. His fingers stroked and aroused her, and then they were gone.

"Miklo?" she whispered, then heard him tearing open one of the foil packages.

"I want to be gentle, but I don't know if I can." His voice was tense and urgent.

"I need you," she said, and pulled him over her. "Nothing else matters." The heat of him strained at her feminine core, and she stiffened as unwanted memories flooded her, making her scrunch her eyes closed.

"Just relax, darling," he said, and cupped her face in his hand. "Look at me. Keep your eyes on me."

When she raised her gaze to his, all she found was desire for her in his eyes. His hand bent her leg at the knee as he pressed against her flesh.

"Miklo."

"You are beautiful."

With his hands tight on her hips, he eased into her. Never had she been filled so completely. "Oh," she gasped as he entered her fully.

Miklo mumbled a mixture of Greek and Spanish, his breath hot in her ear as he withdrew from her and plunged deep inside again and again. Unable to think any more, she gave in to the demands of her body and let Miklo take her wherever he wanted to go. Paradise was just a moment away.

The honey wetness of her body clung to him, and he almost exploded the second he entered her. Seeking to ease the pressure, he withdrew, but his body had other plans, and he sheathed himself deeply within her again. Each stroke took him closer to completion, but he wanted to please Jeannine first. Trembling, he eased back to sit on his heels and wrapped her long legs around his hips. One hand drifted to where their bodies were joined, and he let his thumb stroke over her female bud. Buried deep within her, he listened to the demands of his body and closed his eyes.

Jeannine clasped the blankets in her fists and tried not to cry out. The feel of him inside her and the magic his hands created on her flesh were too much to bear. Assaulted on all sides by him, she could no longer hold back and allowed the instinct within her to take over.

Surrendering completely to Miklo, her hips moved to match the rhythm he set, and she reached for her release. With one final touch, Miklo took her over the edge, and she cried out as the fire consumed her. Miklo leaned over top of her as her body clamped down on his flesh. Hurrying the pace, he urged her on, drawing out her orgasm until he gripped her hips tightly, no longer able to control himself. Deep inside her, his body found the sanctuary it had so desperately craved.

Long minutes passed as she held his trembling body in her embrace, arms locked around his shoulders and legs tight around his hips. The spasms of his body finally ceased, and he pulled back to kiss her.

"Jeannine," he whispered, and kissed her deeply. "You are glorious."

Tears pricked her eyes at his words. In that moment she knew she loved him.

As the night deepened, Jeannine later woke to Miklo's roused body behind her. They lay spoon fashion and the heat of his firm flesh between her thighs stirred her body to its new awakening. A tingle pulsed from her core, and moisture flooded her feminine sheath. Lord, she was ready for him in seconds now that her body knew what to do, knew what to anticipate, knew what it wanted.

Miklo gently pressed the tip of his erection against her moist flesh. With him whispering gentle words behind her, she trusted him, trusted him with her body and so much more.

Instinct took over, and she pressed back into him. "Easy, love, easy," he said as he entered her from behind. Each touch of him surged her forward to completion. Nothing had ever felt as good as Miklo's touch. With his muscled arm a band around her waist, he controlled her body, and they moved in unison. Arching back, she pressed into him urgently, her undefined need taking over. This was what she had wanted, what she had needed, and she gave herself completely to him.

The night waned as Jeannine twined her body with Miklo's, and they slept, tangled together.

Miklo tried not to wake her, but the second he moved, she woke.

"Miklo?" she said, and reached out to him. "Are you going?"

"Yes. It's still early. You should go back to sleep for a while." He pressed a kiss to her forehead and tucked the sheet around her.

"Is everything okay?" she asked, her sleepy eyes focusing on him in the dim light.

"Roberto's got a fever again with new jaw pain. He might be developing an infection or an abscess, so I need to go and see him."

She threw her feet over the edge of the bed and sat. "I'm coming, too. I'm sorry, I didn't hear your phone."

"It's okay. I'm sorry I woke you." He kissed her nose, liking the sleepy look of her. "The life of a surgeon, you know. I have to go, but I'll call you later."

"Wait. I'd really like to come."

"Are you ready for that?" he asked, and stroked her hair back.

"What do you mean?" Anxiety stirred in her.

"I mean, I got the call at five in the morning. If we both show up looking sleepy-eyed together, people will assume things about us."

"Oh," she said, and plopped down on the bed as her brain woke fully to what he was really saying. "I see what you mean."

"I don't want to put you in that position."

"I couldn't care less what people think about me. I'm more concerned about you."

"I'm…not sure that either of us is ready for that."

Searching his eyes, she didn't find any answers. She didn't have any either. "Will you call me and let me know how he is?"

"I will."

"Maybe I'll go in and check on him in a couple of hours."

"That's a good idea. He'll love that."

"Gives me time to drop by the store and get him a new car, too."

Miklo grinned, then his throat suddenly went tight with emotion. With a nod, he turned and walked away before he couldn't.

Hours later, Jeannine woke to the phone ringing in her ear. She debated whether to answer it, but the darned thing kept ringing, so she reached for it.

"Hello?" she said, and threw her arm over her eyes. She really didn't want to be awake yet.

"Is Dr. Hottie still there?" Trish's voice made her open her eyes.

"Trish!"

"Did you get my present?" Trish asked with a laugh.

"Yes, thank you. It was very unexpected." Jeannine nodded and relaxed against the pillows with Miklo's scent surrounding her.

"I thought you might like it. Did…everything…go okay?"

"Yes. It was wonderful," she whispered. "I didn't know making love could be so wonderful."

"I'm really glad. He's a dream."

"And he dances like it, too."

"You're making me jealous, Jeannine."

Jeannine took in a shaky breath, overwhelmed by the events of the past day. "Nothing like this has ever happened to me. I don't quite know how to feel." So many emotions had cracked open in the last twenty-four hours that she was still confused.

"Take a deep breath and enjoy it. Well, I'm going to let you go now. I'm sure you have some things you need to do today."

"Yeah. And thanks again. You're such a good friend."

"See you tomorrow."

"Okay." Jeannine hung up and rose to shower and dress. She wanted to go see Roberto this morning. Seeing Miklo would just be a side bonus. Shorts and a T-shirt were about all she needed for a quick trip to the hospital. As she reached for a long-sleeved shirt to put on over the top, she paused. Glancing down at her arms and the visible scars, the cringe she usually felt coming on didn't happen. Moving to the mirror in the bathroom she looked at herself. Other than needing her hair combed, she looked pretty much like any other person in the morning.

The scars had faded over the last months, but were still clearly visible. Miklo had told her about some lotions that could reduce the scarring and visibility. She knew he'd only been trying to make her feel better, that there was truly no way to fully eliminate the marks. But, hey, who knew? Maybe they would work a little.

Deciding to not worry about anything today, she pulled her hair back into a ponytail and headed for the hospital, quickly stopping at the store on the way.

As she entered the busy building, people rushed by her, jostled her a little, but no one pulled away, disgusted by her appearance, and some of the confidence that she had had in the past returned. The smile that lingered on her face had less to do with having a lovely weekend with Miklo and more to do with finding the joy that had once lived inside her.

After taking the elevator to the PICU, she pushed the double doors open and made her way to Roberto's room. She clipped her hospital badge onto her shirt so that the nurse knew she wasn't an outside visitor. She knocked on the doorway. "Hi. Can I see Roberto?" she asked.

"Hello," the nurse said, and turned around. "Oh, hi!

Didn't recognize you at first out of scrubs. I'm Charlene," she said, and shook Jeannine's hand. "You're one of the new nurses, right?"

"Yes, I am." Her quick glance caught the heart monitor and then moved to Roberto on the bed. "How's he doing? Is he still febrile?" She stepped closer. "I have a little present for him if he's awake."

"He's in and out with a little sedation, but thankfully the ventilator tubing is removed now."

"Oh, that's fabulous. When did that happen?"

"Early this morning, I think. He was doing so well that Miklo extubated him and put him on simple oxygen." Charlene shook her head in amazement. "He's sure a fighter."

Jeannine withdrew a yellow car from her purse and placed it on the bed. "I don't want to wake him, but will you tell him I stopped by and brought him a new car so that we can race?"

"I sure will," Charlene said with a laugh.

Jeannine lingered at the door for a moment and then headed for the nurses' station.

CHAPTER THIRTEEN

MIKLO scribbled the last note in the last chart of the last patient he wanted to see that day. He glanced at the clock on the wall. Still time to call Jeannine. Though they had been awake for most of the night, he felt no fatigue, and his thoughts had drifted to her continuously throughout the day. What weighed heavily on his mind was that his time with Jeannine gave him a sense of peace that had been lacking for so long. Peace he had never had with his wife. Though he'd grown to love her, he hadn't craved her with the same kind of passion he seemed to have developed for Jeannine.

Flopping back against the chair, he thought about her. About last night. About what it meant. About what it could mean.

Before he could wrap his brain around that idea, his phone rang.

"Dr. Kyriakides."

"Miklo!" his uncle almost yelled into his ear. "Come to Olympia's at four and bring your nurse. We're celebrating."

"What are we celebrating?" he asked, amused. With his uncle, he never knew.

"Christo is finally graduating, and I don't have to pay for any more college."

As he listened to his uncle, the object of his fascination approached the nurses' station. Though focused on her, he gave a short laugh into the phone. "That is something to celebrate. I'll ask her, she just walked up."

"Just bring her. Be here at four or you'll be in trouble with your auntie. She was sorry she missed you last time."

"I am, too." They spoke another minute, and then Miklo rang off. "Good afternoon, Miss Carlyle."

"Afternoon, Dr. Kyriakides."

"You're looking mighty fetching today." He let his gaze roll down her bare legs and back up again to her arms.

"Fetching?" She laughed and sat in a chair beside him. "I haven't heard that term in a long time."

"It seems the most appropriate description. You're not bothered without a longer-sleeved shirt?" he asked.

"Amazingly enough, no. The need to cover myself has begun to fade." She held her arms up and examined them as if they were something new to her. "I'm going to try the creams you recommended as well."

"Excellent." She was healing right in front of him.

"How are you today?"

"That was going to be my question to you, and what are you doing here on your weekend off?"

She shrugged. "I wanted to see how Roberto was

doing." She nodded at the phone still in his hand. "You got a phone call that involved me somehow?"

"What?" He looked at the phone and then stuck it in his pocket. "Yes. My uncle wants us to come to a party this afternoon." Miklo leaned closer and the clean fragrance of her almost made his mouth water. "He's very insistent that you come, but I told him I would *ask* if you'd *like* to come."

The smile on her face started in her eyes, tilting the corners up. "I'd like that. But are you sure you want me along for a family function? I mean…" Her gaze darted away, her discomfort obvious.

"He specifically asked that you come, and he'll have my hide if I don't bring you." Then Miklo realized how that could be interpreted, and he could have kicked himself for being such a verbal klutz. He really did want her with him. It finally seemed like the right place, the right time, and…the right woman. "Jeannine, I know that sounded stupid, but I would like you to come."

"It's okay. I understand. I'd love to come," she said with a laugh and then glanced around, as if realizing they were sitting in a very public place.

"So what's Roberto's condition? I saw that you extubated him." She adjusted her position to a more upright one and cleared her throat.

Good. Talk about work would keep his attention off of Jeannine's long, long, legs and what they had done to him last night. "He was more than ready. Even though he's still running a slight fever, he was doing well enough to extubate him. I did lance a small abscess in his jaw and sent it for culture." Miklo stood and shoved the chart back into its rack. His job here was done. "I was about to head out. I can walk you out if you'd like."

Jeannine nodded, and looked around, realizing that they were getting a little attention from the staff. "I did just come in about Roberto," she said, her eyes cautious once again.

"I know." He walked beside her through the double doors back into the hallway and away from the staff who could turn a casual conversation into a disclosure of national secrets by the end of a shift. Starting gossip about Jeannine was something he certainly didn't want to do. He didn't care so much about himself as he did about protecting her.

"So, what's the occasion this evening?" she asked.

"Christo is finally graduating from university. But with my family, any excuse to get together is a good one." He gave a smile, then frowned as a twinge in his chest caught him by surprise.

"What's wrong?"

"I hadn't realized until now, just how much I've missed that. The spontaneous get-togethers, the camaraderie of the family, the unbelievable amount of food." His mouth watered at the thought and his anticipation skyrocketed. Seeing his family again was going to be great. Having Jeannine with him was going to be even better.

Jeannine paused in the hallway and placed her hand on his arm. He'd not worn his labcoat today and the warmth of her skin was a pleasant reminder of last night and how fantastic their skin had felt together.

"Don't feel bad about missing something you want or need in your life, Miklo. We all need our family, our friends, our support system. If you want to go alone tonight, I won't be offended."

She was such a gem. Her insight was one of the most attractive things about her. Another thing he hadn't realized he'd needed in his life.

Miklo frowned, unsure of himself as he looked down into her soft gaze. "Jeannine, I have a confession to make," he said, and couldn't believe that he was going to say this, but every word was true.

"I'm almost afraid to ask," she said with a cringe. "What is it?"

"I thought about you all day long." Though he had focused on his patients when he'd had to, thoughts of Jeannine and last night had stolen his attention every other moment. The warmth of a new pulse was present with every beat of his heart. Jeannine was responsible for putting it there.

She gave a shaky laugh and her eyes betrayed her emotions. "I thought a lot about you, too."

"That's very good. Why don't I pick you up in an hour or so? Dress casual. We'll go have a nice dinner, catch up with the family, and then who knows what."

"I'll be ready," she said. Miklo watched as she made her way down the hall toward the employee elevators.

In an hour, Miklo knocked on her door. Insides trembling, palms damp, he felt like a kid on his first date again as he pushed the hair back from his face. When Jeannine opened the door and offered him a welcoming smile, he felt as if she had opened the door to his heart. Emotions he hadn't acknowledged in years suddenly flooded through him, almost dropping him to his knees. The pain that had squeezed his heart for too long eased, and he could breathe again.

When she opened the door he charged inside, took her in his arms and held her against him until the trembling stopped.

"Miklo?" she asked as she hugged him back. "Are you okay?"

The feel of her trim body against him was what he needed. Pulling back slightly, he found her lips and kissed her thoroughly as his body prepared for much more than a simple embrace. Cupping his hands around her face, he placed a tender kiss on her mouth and looked into her blue-green eyes, which suddenly filled with a sheen of moisture.

"I've wanted to do that all day long. I'm sorry I couldn't stay this morning." He searched her eyes for anger or disappointment, but found none. "Last night was wonderful."

Clasping her hands tight on his wrists, she held him closer. "It was. Thank you."

"You have no idea how beautiful you are, do you?" He pushed a stray strand of hair back from her face.

"Me? I've...never thought of myself that way. Especially not after—"

"Shh." Groaning, it took everything he had to take a step away from her, but for both their sakes he had to. "You are." Succumbing to her charm and abandoning the party tonight would be entirely too easy to do. "How about I tell you about who we're going to meet on the way?" Distraction. That was the ticket. Lots of distraction so he could keep his hands off of her.

"Go ahead, but I'm warning you, I'm terrible with names." She took a shaky breath and picked up her purse.

"That's okay. Just smile and nod and call most of the men Christo."

In less than twenty minutes they arrived at the restaurant crowded with his family.

"I think there are more people here now than when we came here the first time," Jeannine said as they pushed through the doorway.

"Miklo! Jeannine!" Seferino called from across the room and made his way through the crowd to them. Before he reached Miklo, he reached out to kiss Jeannine on both cheeks. "I'm so glad you could come." He held onto Jeannine's hand and led the way back through the crowd, leaving an astonished Miklo to follow along behind.

Hours later, having met countless cousins, aunts, and uncles and eaten the most outrageously wicked food she'd ever seen, Jeannine collapsed into a chair at a corner table. The glass of iced water in her hand was refreshing and after talking so long, she certainly needed it.

Glancing around the room, she looked for Miklo and found him engaged in conversation with another man about his age. She watched as they chatted, admiring what a handsome man he was. But she knew that her attraction for him was so much more than his physical appearance. He cared about people, he cared about helping others, and he appeared to care about her. Jeannine swallowed as he looked up and met her gaze.

Her life had changed so much in the last six months. She'd almost died, and now here she was with the man of her dreams looking at her as if he wanted to take a bite out of her.

A woman with dark hair that was graying sat across the table from Jeannine. They had been introduced some time ago and Jeannine remembered that this was Miklo's Aunt Jolanda, Seferino's wife. "How are you, Jeannine?" she asked, and poured more water. "Did you get enough to eat?"

"Oh, my, yes," Jeannine said with a pat to her stomach. "I won't have to eat for days."

"Bah. You're too thin. You need to eat more," Jolanda said, and patted Jeannine's hand.

"I've been ill in the last year, and I'm still trying to gain back the weight I lost over it." Jeannine didn't know how much to tell the woman. Would she think badly of her if she knew the whole story?

"Miklo told his uncle and he told me that you were hospitalized and almost died." Her large brown eyes grew serious and she clucked her tongue in sympathy. "I'm just glad you're better and are spending time with Miklo. He needs a good friend, too."

"He…told me about his wife," Jeannine said.

"It was a tragedy." Her shrug said it all. "But life goes on, and we must go on with it."

Jeannine gave a tearful laugh at the woman's insight. "You are so right."

Jolanda stood and gave Jeannine a quick hug. "Now I have to start cleaning up."

"Would you like some help? I'd be glad to."

"Oh, no. I couldn't ask—"

"You're not asking, I'm volunteering," Jeannine said. "I'll bring dishes to the kitchen and you can tell me where to put things."

Jolanda patted Jeannine's cheek. "You're a good-hearted woman. Just what he needs."

Before Jeannine could digest that, Jolanda scurried away into the kitchen.

Jeannine gathered dishes from a number of tables and took them to the kitchen, where Jolanda directed her to the dishwasher. Miklo entered the kitchen behind her. "What are you doing?" he asked, and observed her from the doorway as Jolanda returned to the dining room.

"The dishes. What does it look like?" she said, and tossed a white towel at him with a laugh. "And you can help."

He caught the towel before it hit him in the face. "Me? I'm a highly trained surgeon. I can't take the chance of damaging my hands," he said with a self-satisfied smile.

"Sissy."

Brows raised in disbelief, he took a step toward her. "What?"

Jeannine dunked an armload of dishes into a pan of sudsy water. "You heard me," she said. Though she kept her gaze on her task, she knew the precise moment he stood behind her. The thread of desire that shot through her made her weak in the knees.

With a gentle hand, he brushed the hair back over her

shoulder. "Thank you," he said, his voice soft as he kissed her temple, his fragrance washing over her.

"For what?" she asked, startled as she leaned into his kiss.

"For everything." Turning her, he brought her face up for his kiss. Against her will, her sudsy hands reached out to his shoulders and she clung to him.

Seferino was about to enter the kitchen with a tray loaded with dirty dishes.

"Stop!" Jolanda screeched, and grabbed him by the waist. "You can't go in there."

"Why not? It's where the dirty dishes go."

Jolanda hushed him with an impatient wave of her hand. "Miklo is in there."

"It's about time he did some dishes. Let me bring him some more."

"That's not all he's doing."

"The floors, too? Good man." Seferino reached out to push the door open with one hand. Jolanda tugged on his sleeve again.

"No! *Jeannine* is in there with him." Seferino set the tray down on a nearby table. The two huddled at the door and peeked through the window.

"You can come in now," Miklo said, and backed away from Jeannine. He wiped the kitchen towel over his face.

Seferino picked up the tray of dishes and brought them in. "Are you going to help with the dishes, too?"

Miklo's gaze fastened onto Jeannine. "I think I will."

* * *

Miklo paused in the ER hallway before heading home. Being here reminded him of his days as a resident, a time of high energy, a lust for life and his work, a feeling that nothing coming through those doors was beyond his abilities. Now he didn't crave the lifestyle any longer. He much preferred his duties in the PICU, a more controlled setting, more conducive to a home life, though he didn't really have one.

The stairwell door opened and Jeannine walked out, with her backpack slung over one shoulder, obviously ready to head home, too. She hesitated a moment when she saw him. "Hi, Miklo. How are you?" she asked, her pace slowing. She paused at the exit door, her gaze searching his.

In the short time he'd known her, he'd realized that they had become friends. He'd missed that companionship and until now he hadn't realized how much he'd needed it. He needed to talk to someone, someone who knew what his work life was like and could commiserate with him about cases. Someone who understood him. That hadn't explained why his hands shook when he saw her. Why his heart beat erratically when he was near her. Three days had passed since the party at Olympia's and he'd missed seeing her.

"Jeannine, I—"

"Help! I need help!" a female voice cried from outside the exit door.

Jeannine and Miklo dashed out to find a distraught woman in the door of the ambulance bay.

"What's wrong?" Jeannine asked, and tried to lead the woman inside. "Are you hurt?"

"No, my sister. She collapsed." The woman dashed out of the door to a car, with Miklo, Jeannine and other staff racing after her.

"Someone get a gurney," Jeannine instructed.

Miklo saw a woman slumped over in the passenger side of the car. He jerked open the door and pain sliced through his heart.

"She's pregnant," the woman said, as tears poured from her eyes. "Please help her."

Sweat and memories poured over Miklo at the sight of the unconscious woman. Without thought, he reached in a scooped the heavily pregnant woman into his arms. She didn't rouse at the movement.

"Put her on the stretcher," Jeannine said, and reached out to hold the woman's head upright.

"Don't touch her," Miklo said, his voice rough. He took a step back from Jeannine.

"Dr. Kyriakides," Jeannine said strongly. "Put her on the gurney, and we'll take her inside."

Miklo complied with a nod as his heart raced out of control. A male attendant took one end of the stretcher and Jeannine took the other, while Miklo hurried alongside. "Trauma One," Miklo said, and directed the gurney there. Staff had already set up the room. A respiratory therapist placed oxygen over the patient's face, another nurse started an IV, and Jeannine applied the heart and fetal monitors.

"Tell me what happened to her," Miklo instructed the distraught woman.

"We were at the mall, shopping for baby clothes. She said she had a headache and was tired. She took an aspirin, and we stopped to rest." The woman shrugged. "She seemed okay for a while and then when we were in the car she fainted. Is she okay? Is she going to be all right?"

"What's her name?" Miklo asked and flashed his penlight across the woman's pupils.

"Maria Romero."

"Thank you for bringing her in." Concentrating on the patient, Miklo barely looked up.

"She's had headaches for weeks and took a lot of aspirin, but we all thought it was just from hormones or something, you know?"

"Why don't you call her husband to come in?" Jeannine asked, knowing they'd need him here soon if the woman didn't respond.

"Is she gonna die?" the woman shrieked, and clutched Miklo's arm.

"No. I don't know yet. She just needs to have her husband with her. He needs to be here." Miklo gave the woman's shoulder a squeeze and returned to Maria's side. "One pupil is blown, the other is sluggish." He stood upright and faced the staff in the room. "Radiology. Now. I'll call Neurosurgery on the way," Miklo said, and pulled out his cellphone.

"You think it's an aneurysm or a stroke?" Jeannine asked as they rounded the corner to the radiology department.

"AVM. Happens sometimes in pregnancy."

"I'm not familiar with that term."

"Arterial-venous malformation. An irregularity at a junction in the vessels of the brain. The pressure of the cardiovascular system in pregnancy causes it to expand and then rupture at the weak point."

"Oh, God," she said as they rolled Maria into the CAT scanner room.

Miklo dialed a number on his phone. "Joshua? Where are you? It's Miklo." After listening to the response, he nodded. "I've got a pregnant woman, possible AVM. We're in CAT scan right now. Scrub, and we'll be in the OR in ten minutes."

"We need to hurry," Jeannine whispered. "There are decelerations on the fetal monitor. We need to move, or we're going to lose them both."

Miklo grabbed the phone on the wall and dialed the hospital emergency system. "Obstetrical emergency team to the OR." He slammed the phone down. "Let's go." Miklo was more determined than ever to save this mother and her child.

"She's far enough along that the baby can probably be saved," Jeannine said.

Miklo avoided looking at Jeannine, but concentrated on putting one foot in front of the other in the race to the OR to save this woman.

Within minutes several events occurred. Miklo and Jeannine turned the patient over to the neurosurgery team, the obstetrical team and newborn ICU teams arrived to perform an emergency Cesarean surgery to save the baby, and the newborn ICU team placed a squalling baby boy into the arms of his father, who broke down and wept.

Miklo left the OR, pain vibrating through him.

Two hours later Jeannine found Miklo staring through the window of the newborn nursery. For a few moments she stood beside him, waiting, watching, hoping.

"Miklo?" Though she wanted to reach out to him, she hesitated to pull him from his silent musings. "Are you okay?"

Without answering, he continued to stare at the activity in the nursery for a few minutes. Then he sighed and seemed to withdraw even more. "I don't think I can do this any more."

"Do what?" Though it struck fear in her heart, she had to know, had to ask.

"This." He nodded at the window. "Watch people die."

"But this one didn't die. You saved them both, didn't you know that?" She touched his arm, making sure that he saw her, felt her.

"I happened to be in the right place at the right time."

"Exactly. If you hadn't been there, they would have both died, and that man with a baby in his arms would have lost everything." Tears flooded her eyes as she watched helplessly at Miklo pushing her silently away.

Miklo faced her, angry frustration blazing in his eyes. "Come on, Jeannine—"

"No, Miklo, you come on. This is where you needed

to be, when you needed to be here. Do you think that family is any less grateful than you would have been had the circumstances been different?" She dragged in a breath, trying to control the emotions about to spill out of her. "You saved a woman, her unborn child, and gave them back to their family. That's not a gift to be taken lightly. You know that, Miklo."

Miklo calmed and met her gaze, saw truth in her eyes. At least, the truth as she believed it. Could he take that truth of hers and live with it, make it his own? Somehow he doubted it. His life, his jaded attitude was too far gone. He'd had a brief interlude into the light of what Jeannine offered, but it wasn't enough to keep him there, wasn't enough to make him whole again. She deserved more than half a man to love her, to fully love her, not the half way he had done.

"I know you're hurting right now, but you have to let them go." Her lips trembled, and he wanted to reach out to smooth them into a smile, but his hands remained at his sides. "It's the only way for you to survive. To live again."

Miklo unclenched his fists and tunneled his hands into her hair, dragging her close against him, not caring where they were or who witnessed the downward spiral of his life. This was the last time he was going to touch Jeannine.

Jeannine's arms clutched around his waist. "Hang onto me, Miklo. Hang onto me as long as you can."

"You're a wonderful woman, Jeannine." His throat was tight, his tongue thick in his mouth. The effort to suppress his emotions choked him.

"Don't you dare give me that."

"I mean it. These last few weeks have been wonderful because of you. You're bright, you're beautiful, compassionate and smart."

"But?"

"I don't think I can do this again."

"Do what?"

"Lose someone the way I lost my family, the way Maria was almost lost to her family." Though he wasn't related to her, though he didn't know the family, the situation was too close to home for him to just let go of it so easily. Reason and logic had no place here. "I didn't love Darlene the way… Losing her almost killed me. If something happened to you, too, I don't know if I could bear it. At least if I walk away now I know you'll be safe."

"Miklo. There are no guarantees in life. Just chances. If you're not willing to take a chance, then I don't know what we can do."

The sound of her voice in his head made him want to let go, let go of everything that had been holding him back, but he couldn't. The ability to take that step and keep going had somehow been blocked by the pain of the past, the pain that would never let him go.

He pulled back and released her. He turned away, unable to bear the worry, the concern, the love in her eyes. He knew she loved him. Every step they had taken together had brought them closer, and she had fallen over the edge. It was in her touch, in her kiss, in every breath she took when she was with him. And it was his fault that she was hurting so badly.

"I'm very concerned about you."

"I'm so sorry I've dragged you down with me. Hurting you was never my intention."

"Miklo, you deserve to be happy, no matter who you choose to be with. Spending your life paying for a mistake that wasn't yours is just plain wrong. No one should give up their life for such a thing." She grabbed his sleeve. "Accidents and tragedies happen. They are part of life. We've both suffered long enough, and we deserve to be happy."

He thought of her and the pregnancy that had almost ended her life. They had both lost a child. She hadn't given up, she had survived and persevered, changed her life, and was now a success. "You are one of the bravest people I have ever met in my life."

"I'm not brave, just too stubborn to quit." Her watery gaze held his.

She gave him a sad smile that made his heart lurch. Taking two steps back from her, he shoved his hands into his pockets. "Something is broken in me, Jeannine, and I don't know how to fix it."

"If you'll let me, I can help you."

"You already have." Miklo took another step back from her. Needing the space between them for a moment before he broke down and took her in his arms again. "I'm sorry, but I need some time right now."

Jeannine looked away, sniffed and nodded. "I understand."

And she knew it was over between them. Recovering from devastating events was impossible for some people. Miklo might never recover, even though he'd made an attempt.

Closing the gap between them in two strides, he cupped her face in his hands and pressed a hard kiss against her mouth. "I'm sorry." Seconds later, he released her and walked away.

CHAPTER FOURTEEN

RATHER than waiting by the phone like a teenager who'd been dumped by her boyfriend, Jeannine worked as many shifts as she could and kept herself busy. Miklo hadn't called her since the night they had spoken outside the nursery window, just a few days ago. He might call her, he might not. She understood that, accepted it, and she resisted the temptation to call him. It didn't stop her from looking up and hoping every time she saw an attending physician with dark hair come into the lounge for a cup of coffee. Their time together was probably over.

"So, how's Dr. Hottie these days?" Trish asked as they entered the break room.

Jeannine reached for the coffee-pot and poured them both a cup before she answered. "I'm…not sure."

"What do you mean?" Trish demanded, and sat straight upright in her chair, her eyes bright with suspicion.

"It's that simple." She stirred creamer in her coffee and watched the black liquid swirl into an amber color. "He's busy. I'm busy," she said with a shrug, and tried to look casual about it.

"Did something happen that you're not telling me?"

The concern in Trish's voice was almost enough to bring tears to Jeannine's eyes, but she resisted the urge to give in to that indulgence. She'd survived much more than heartache, and she wasn't about to give in now. "Maybe we really aren't as compatible as I thought we were."

"But you said the sex was fabulous!"

"It was," she said in a hushed tone, and looked around to see if anyone lingered in the hallway. "Relationships aren't just about sex."

"They're not?" A completely innocent look covered Trish's face as she thought about it. "Oh, dear."

"No, they're not, silly, and you know it." She playfully batted her friend on the arm and released a pent-up giggle. The tension of the day had been heavy, and she needed the release.

"Wow. I'm glad you straightened me out on that one. No telling how long I could have gone on having fabulous sex with someone thinking I was having a *relationship*." Trish chuckled and sipped her coffee, then she leaned forward in her seat. "So what do you think happened between you and Miklo?"

"I don't know. He's had a devastating past and it may take a lot more than someone like me for him to get over it."

"What do you mean, *someone like you?*" Trish narrowed her eyes at Jeannine.

Uncomfortable, Jeannine switched positions in her chair, but it didn't help. "I mean…someone more attractive, someone Greek."

"You'd better rethink that, you're talking about my friend. Although you can't overcome not being Greek, there's nothing else wrong with you that a little confidence won't cure."

Jeannine told Trish about the pregnant patient that she and Miklo had cared for and how it related to his past. "You know as well as I do that something like that can trigger past emotions that we haven't dealt with. It's painful, it tears you up inside, but then you move on. He'll get there. He just needs a little space."

Jeannine wished that Trish's words were really true, but she knew better. Somehow she had deluded herself about Miklo, and her denial had come to an abrupt end.

"I think I'm going to go see Roberto. He's going to go home in a few days, so I'd better see him now." Jeannine finished her coffee and stood.

"Jeannine," Trish said and reached out to her friend. "I'm so sorry."

"Yeah, me, too."

Miklo finished his rounds and looked at his watch. After placing a note in the chart, he looked at the clock on the wall. Time had seemed to stand still for him the last few days. Funny how it had flown when he had been with Jeannine. He hadn't been fair to her, and he needed to call her. He owed her an apology. And just maybe she would forgive him.

Then his pager went off and an overhead page followed seconds later. "Any doctor to the ER. Any doctor to the ER."

That was always a bad sign.

He raced down the stairs, taking them three at a time and leaping onto the landing. He burst through the ER doorway into pure chaos.

Staff scattered in all directions and at least ten police officers scuffled with several prisoners in orange jumpsuits.

"Hold it right there," one of the cops said, and tried to push him back into the stairwell. "We have a hostile situation here."

"I'm a physician here. Where's the emergency?" he asked, and caught his breath, trying to see through the mob of struggling prisoners and police. "There was a distress page overhead."

"Don't know. We got our hands full with this lot. Tried to overtake the prison bus and ended up wrecking it instead. There are more on the way."

"Let me through," Miklo said as a sick feeling of dread curled in his gut. Where was Jeannine today? He hoped she was safely in the PICU, but if there had been a call for help, he knew she would have come. Something was seriously wrong here, and he rushed toward the nurses' station. Voices, shouting, and chaos where there normally was controlled urgency made his concern turn to worry. As he neared the nursing station he swallowed hard and skidded to a halt.

Jeannine lay sprawled on the floor, covered in blood, holding an unconscious Trish in her arms.

Miklo dropped to the floor beside them and tried to keep his heart from pounding out of his chest. "Are you okay? What happened?" he asked, and struggled to get the penlight out of his pocket.

"I'm okay, but Trish is really hurt." She gave a gasp and made a visible attempt to control the tremor of her lower lip. "We got called to help. The prisoners were in a big mob, fighting. They ran right over her and knocked her into me. I think they broke her nose and maybe her jaw," she said as she continued to cup a hand along Trish's face, which was swollen and starting to bruise. Although tears flowed from her eyes and her voice cracked, Jeannine maintained her professionalism under the deepest stress.

"Has she responded at all?" he asked, as he shone the flashlight in Trish's pupils.

"No, she's been out about four or five minutes. Are her pupils okay?" she asked, and her blue-green gaze clung to him.

"Yes. We need to get her to Radiology if those men are contained." He stood and looked down the hallway. The police and prisoners had exploded out into the parking lot, and only a few remained inside. Some sat quietly in chairs lining the hallway and the police tending them appeared alert to any changes. Miklo bent down to Jeannine again. "Let's get her onto a gurney, get oxygen and suction, and we'll take her straight away."

Jeannine sniffed back a tear and nodded. "She needs a neck collar before we move her." She looked up at the male assistant hovering protectively nearby. "Can you get me a collar and bring a stretcher?"

He dug into a cupboard overhead and handed Miklo the collar. "Here. I'll be right back." Then he raced off and returned seconds later with a stretcher. "Let us help you. She's too heavy for you to pick up by yourself."

Miklo carefully applied the neck collar to Trish while she still lay in Jeannine's arms. "I'll take her shoulders," Miklo said, and gently moved the unconscious woman from Jeannine's arms into his own. "Sweetheart, can you stabilize her head as we move?"

"Yes," Jeannine said. She crouched beside them, and placed her hands on Trish's head. "Ready. Count of three." Other staff members moved in to help as well now that the immediate threat was resolving. The atmosphere of the ER had turned solemn as concern for a co-worker took precedence over everything else.

"One…two…three," Miklo said.

Together they lifted the unconscious nurse off the floor and placed her gently on the gurney.

Miklo touched Jeannine on the shoulder as they made their way through the crowded hallway to Radiology. "She's going to be okay. I may have to take her to surgery, but she's going to be okay."

Tears flooded those beautiful eyes, and her chin trembled. "Thank you, Miklo," she whispered as they hurried away from the ER.

Two days later Trish opened her bruised and swollen eyes for the first time. Jeannine was seated at her side and began to cry.

"You cried when she was unconscious. Now you're

crying that she's waking up," Miklo said, and shook his head with a teasing smile. "Some women just can't be satisfied."

Trish gave an indignant snort, and then winced beneath the bandages that covered the lower part of her face.

"Are you in pain?" Miklo asked her, and began to remove a piece of gauze.

Slowly Trish nodded.

"That'll teach you to disagree with your doctor," he said, but there was no heat behind the words. "We'll get you something a little stronger now that we know you're going to be waking up with an attitude."

Jeannine sat on the other side of the bed and took Trish's hand. "Your jaw is wired, so you can't talk right now. Miklo said it's only for a while. And your nose was broken, but he fixed that, too."

Trish squeezed her hand tight around Jeannine's and tears escaped her eyes.

"Do you remember anything?" she asked.

Trish shook her head.

With a sigh, Jeannine filled her in on the details of the event that had put her in hospital as a patient instead of a nurse.

Miklo listened to Jeannine's soft voice as she filled in the missing details in Trish's memory. He busied himself checking the dressings and assessing the suture lines, but everything was fine.

"There are several small sutures that will have to come out in a few weeks, but your surgeon did an excellent job, and they are almost invisible," Miklo said.

Jeannine gave a watery laugh and dabbed at her eyes with a tissue. "Your surgeon is very humble, don't you think?"

"I'm glad you've decided to wake up. If you had stayed out any longer I was going to get worried. You took quite a wallop to the head, but nothing nasty showed up on CAT scan or MRI. Just a very severe concussion."

Trish gave a thumbs-up sign, then let her arm drop onto the bed.

"She's exhausted," Jeannine said. "I think we need to get out of here and let her sleep."

"Good idea." Miklo followed her out of Trish's room. Jeannine looked up at Miklo. Emotions that he didn't want to have burned the back of his throat. He swallowed hard and pushed them back down where they belonged.

"Thank you for everything you've done for her." Jeannine placed her hand on his arm. "I've missed you."

She turned away from him and it was all he could do not to reach out to her, not pull her into his arms and not admit to her the things he'd been feeling. He's missed her presence at his side. It was that simple. Her humor, the way she didn't take herself too seriously, and the glow of her eyes when she looked at him.

Though she wasn't Greek, had not one drop of Mediterranean blood in her, there had been enough tragedy in her life to more than make up for it. The Greeks and Romans hadn't cornered the market on sorrow.

* * *

Over the next several days, Jeannine spent as much time as possible with Trish. Utilizing a dry erase board, they were able to communicate, but mostly Trish listened to Jeannine recall interesting patients that Trish had missed.

On this day, Jeannine pushed a wheelchair into Trish's room. "I've got the car out front. Oh, and I got you a high-power blender. Miklo said you'll still be wired shut for another two to four weeks, so we'll need to puree everything."

Trish sat on the edge of the bed in her pajamas and robe, ready for her discharge home. "Pizza???" she wrote on the board.

"Ew." Jeannine made a face. "Not sure how that will work, but we can give it a whirl, but fruit would probably be better."

"Strawberry Daiquiri?" she wrote with a hopeful expression on her face.

"You're still on antibiotics. They don't mix well with alcohol, and I'm not sure that's the best use of a fruit smoothie."

Trish snorted.

"Ready?"

Trish shrugged, and Jeannine saw the fear in her eyes.

"Don't be scared. I'll be with you, and some of the staff are going to take turns checking in on you when I'm working."

Trish nodded, scribbled on the board and turned it to face Jeannine. "Dr. Hottie."

"No. Miklo and I aren't seeing each other any more. You won't have to worry about him taking up my time, if that's what you're concerned about." She knew it was over. He had made that clear.

Trish shook the board at Jeannine and frowned.

"He can't be with me for a variety of reasons." Jeannine looked at Trish. "It just wasn't meant to be between us, I know that now."

Trish gave a snort and shook her head in disgust. She turned the board over and wrote a new message for Jeannine.

Behind you.

Jeannine's eyes widened and she whirled around to find an amused Miklo leaning in the doorway.

"Spoiler," he said to Trish. "No telling what I might have heard."

"It's not nice to eavesdrop on people," Jeannine said with narrowed eyes, and tried not to react to his unexpected presence. But her heart tripped and her stomach clenched anyway. "What are you doing here?"

"Looking for you," he said softly, the light in his eyes very different than the last time she had seen him.

"Well, I'm not working today. Trish is being discharged, as you know, and I'm taking her home, getting her settled in, and spending every moment I can with her until she gets her jaw unwired."

"You're a good friend." His glance cut to Trish. "Shouldn't be too much longer. I've made an appointment in the office for you for a one-week follow-up. Your prescriptions and discharge instructions are all here." He handed the bundle of papers to Trish.

She took them and placed them on her lap and wrote on the board. "You're an idiot if you don't grab her."

"You're right," Miklo said. "See you in a week."

CHAPTER FIFTEEN

THREE hours later Miklo pulled into Jeannine's driveway, and she tensed. What the heck was he doing here? She'd only come home to get a few things, then she was heading to stay overnight with Trish. She had barely seen him over the last two weeks and had tried to put him from her mind.

Now she trembled as she walked to the door and opened it.

"Hi," he said, and shoved his hands into his pockets.

"Hi." She stood there with her hand on the door. "What are you doing here?"

"I came to see you."

"Why? If something changed in Trish's discharge orders you could have called me."

Miklo frowned and looked away, clearly uncomfortable. "It's not that. I was hoping we could take a tram ride to the top of the mountain, have dinner, and talk a while. Watch the sunset over the mesa."

"That sounds lovely, but I'm spending the night with Trish." She knew Trish would be fine overnight, but right now she was a convenient excuse.

"I see."

"Why don't you just spit out what you want to say to me? You've clearly got something on your mind." Like finishing her off forever.

"I do have something on my mind and had hoped to discuss it with you over dinner." A small smile curve his lips upward.

"Why don't you just do it here? Save yourself a few bucks and don't waste our time." Coldness pierced her heart, aching that Miklo felt the need to confront her this way when he could have just let things fade into nothingness between them.

Now it was his turn to frown. "Do what? I know you don't like flying, but you don't have a fear of the tram, do you?"

"No." She didn't smile, as her heart was breaking into tiny little pieces, though she had known her time with him was going to be limited. "Miklo. You're going to tell me it's over between us, as if I didn't know that already. You don't need to wine and dine me to break it off. I can handle it." But could she really? Would hearing the words come out of his mouth make them any less painful than the speculation had been?

"You can handle it, huh?" he said, and strode closer to her, then closed the door behind him. One silent step at a time brought him face to face with her. His eyes glittered, and she wondered if it was from pain or amusement.

"Isn't that what this is about?"

Slowly Miklo backed her against the wall and braced his hands beside her head, reminding her of the time that he had undressed her here after the Chocolate Fantasy Ball.

The pulse in her throat thrummed and her heartbeat echoed in her ears. Something wasn't right. If he was going to call it off, what was he doing so close to her, looking so hungry for her? Why was his body so hot against hers? And, dammit, why did she have to react so strongly to him?

"*This* is what it's about," he said, and dropped his gaze to her mouth a second before his lips met hers.

Instant fire raced through her. Wild and untamed, it touched the very core of her as Miklo kissed her. Spreading his hands across her hips, he drew her against him, molding her body to his. The heat of him scorched her and made her want to forget a tram ride, dinner, and even Trish.

When he lifted his head, she couldn't believe the desire smoldering in his deep brown eyes.

"Don't play with me, Miklo. That I can't take."

"Did that feel like I was playing?" he asked.

Looking into his eyes, she searched for the truth. "Does this mean you're not dumping me?"

"Yes, I'm not dumping you. But we do have things to talk about and the temptation to strip you naked will be much less if we go someplace public."

"I see." She could still feel the burning flame of his arousal pressed against her, but even she knew that desire was a long way from commitment.

* * *

Jeannine watched the lights of Albuquerque grow smaller and smaller the higher they rose on the twelve-person tram. “How high did the driver say this thing goes again?” she asked, and was glad she couldn’t see the ground below her.

“Don’t be nervous,” Miklo said, and squeezed her shoulder in a gesture of reassurance. “It’s the longest tram in the world, or so the brochure says. The peak of the mountain is over 10,000 feet.” He brought her against his side. “Sitting in the restaurant, looking down the mountain to the west mesa at sunset, is one of my favorite views in the world.”

“That’s saying something, considering how much you’ve traveled.”

“Yeah.” He focused those intense eyes on her. “It’s amazing what you have in your own backyard that you don’t see immediately.”

Jeannine could only imagine what he meant by that statement. The tram swayed in the light breeze blowing through the desert canyon. She was glad it wasn’t any stronger, or the swaying motion would have made her feel ill.

In a few minutes they were settled at a table facing the large windows to the west. “I see what you mean,” she said, and looked out at the magnificent colors across the west mesa. She looked around at the other patrons. Everyone seemed okay, and she gave a quiet chuckle.

“Are you looking for someone?” Miklo asked.

“No. I was just thinking that every time we’ve gone somewhere together there’s been some sort of medical emergency we've gotten dragged into. I'm just waiting for the next one."

Miklo laughed and reached for his water. "That is kind of weird, isn't it? But I don't think we need one tonight."

She leaned forward and motioned him closer. "What do you think of not declaring ourselves next time there's a medical emergency?"

"Somehow I think neither of us would go for that."

"You're right." With a sigh Jeannine looked at Miklo. "I think it's time you tell me why we're here," she said, wishing with all of her heart that things could be different between them. Though she'd known from the beginning that anything between them would be fleeting, it hadn't stopped her from falling in love with him. Sitting here with him now, she was no longer certain, but her lack of confidence in relationships didn't give her any help.

"Tell me what's going on." Her voice was a mere whisper.

"I'm here on a promise."

He reached out for her hand, but for once she derived no comfort from his touch. Inside she was cold, numb to the pain she knew was going to come.

"A promise? What kind of promise? That I won't try to see you any more?" Her heart raced. "That I'll forgo Greek food forever? What?"

"No. This." Withdrawing his hand from hers he fished into his jacket pocket and removed a small box. After placing it on the table, he rose from his chair and lowered himself onto one knee. "This is the promise that started generations ago in my family and one I want to give to you now."

"What are you doing?" she asked, and tried to pull him to his feet, but he remained solidly on one knee beside her, his strength surging through the contact of their skin, straight to her heart. "You don't break up with someone on your knees," she said, and tugged at him one more time.

"No, you don't, which is why I'm in this position." He sighed and his gaze focused intently on her. "For a man to do what I'm about to do, he needs an ability to understand women a little, have a humble spirit, and love in his heart. Until I met you, I didn't know what those were." He brought her hand to his lips and kissed her trembling knuckles.

Tears formed in her eyes as he spoke. No man had ever humbled himself for her. No man had ever understood her, and certainly no man had ever loved her.

"Having known those gifts that only come together once in a lifetime, I don't want them, or you, to ever leave my life." Miklo reached for the box on the table. "This belonged to my great-grandmother." With hands that visibly trembled, he opened the lid to reveal the most stunning wedding set she had ever seen. "I love you, Jeannine. I would be honored if you would wear it and marry me."

"No," she said, and in some part of her numbed mind she heard the patrons around her gasp. Moving from her seat, she knelt on the floor beside him. "I am the one who would be honored to share my life with you." Tears overflowed her eyes as they embraced in the middle of the dining room.

Applause erupted around them, but Jeannine didn't care. "I love you, Miklo." He didn't respond, but the shaking of his body as he held her tight showed her the depth of his emotion. Pulling back, he slipped the ring onto her finger. She laughed as it flopped over.

"I'll have it re-sized, and then it will be perfect on you."

"I love it. It's beautiful. Thank you." Emotions she couldn't name surged through her. Emotions she never thought she'd feel. Emotions she thought that had been long dead inside her now proved how very wrong she had been to allow her dreams to die.

"We're going to have a beautiful life together," Miklo said. He pressed a kiss to her forehead and helped her back into her chair.

"I can't believe you proposed to me!" She took in a few cleansing breaths and pressed her trembling hand to her forehead. "Despite what you said, I really thought you brought me up here to break things off with me."

"You are the brightest light in my life, and I love you. I'm not dumping you ever." He cleared his throat and held her hands in his. "When Darlene died, it nearly killed me. Losing the baby almost finished me off. Two months ago I would have said I didn't need love or another person in my life, but now I know so much better. You helped me more than you'll ever know."

"Miklo, you don't know how badly I want this, how much I want to share my life with you." She hesitated, clenching her fist around the ring and searching his eyes. "But what about children? I don't know whether I can get pregnant, let alone carry one to term. After all that's happened to me, the doctors at the time weren't very encouraging."

"First we need to see what Mother Nature will let your body do before we get too concerned. And, secondly, I don't want to marry you just to have babies. If Mother Nature decides we aren't to have our own family, then we can adopt. There are plenty of children who need a good home, right?" He tucked her hair behind one ear.

"You're right," she whispered as her lip trembled. "I just never wanted to even think about..."

"When the time comes we'll do more than *think* about it," Miklo said, and kissed her.

Jeannine kept her fist clenched to keep the ring on as she threw her arms around Miklo's shoulders and held him tight. "Let's get out of here," she said. Unable to keep her heart from beating madly, she gave in to the happiness that seemed to grow from within her. Miklo was a great part of that, but she'd learned that she could also create her own version of happiness. His presence in her life only made it that much sweeter.

"What did you have in mind?" he asked as they headed for the return tram back down the mountain.

"There's a bottle of champagne waiting in my refrigerator. I think it's time we opened it."

"That's a fabulous idea," he said, and pulled her into an embrace she knew she would never tire of.

EPILOGUE

Two years later

JEANNINE sat at a table at Olympia's restaurant with her feet up on a chair. The water glass beside her remained untouched as she clapped her hands, watching the dancers move around the room. Her eyes were drawn to one particular dancer with wavy dark hair that grazed the collar of his white shirt.

There were many handsome men in the room, but none as attractive as her husband dancing with his three brothers.

She shifted her position on the chair and patted her stomach. "Soon, little one. You'll be dancing with your papa."

At the end of the song, Miklo fell into a chair beside her and drank deeply from the water glass on the table.

"That looked like fun," she said, and handed him her glass of water, too.

"It's great that we're all here," he said between gasping breaths. "I haven't danced so much since our wedding."

"It's good to see you out there with everyone," she said, and absently stroked a hand over her abdomen.

Miklo sat forward and gently cupped her large belly with both hands. "Are you feeling okay still? Not too much exertion?"

"I'm good. Just a little achy in the back and the feet, as usual."

"Do you feel up to dancing with me? They are about to slow things down."

"Are you sure you want to dance with a whale?" Jeannine asked with a laugh. "What if I step on your foot? You'll never be the same again."

"I'll take my chances." Miklo assisted Jeannine to her feet and they walked to the dance floor amid waves and friendly kisses on the cheek and wishes of good luck from many family and friends.

"Let's stay on the edge of the floor in case I need to sit down."

Miklo led her to a corner of the floor and took her in his arms. As they held each other and swayed to the music, Miklo started to shake. Clutching her shoulders as close to him as possible, he held her tight, his emotions running high.

Jeannine held him as tightly as possible, knowing his fears ran deep. Though he had lost one family, he had never forgotten them. Her pregnancy, though wonderful, brought out past pain for both of them. "Everything will be okay, Miklo. It will be fine. The doctor said I'm progressing as I should, and there are no anticipated complications."

"I still worry, love," he said, and kissed her temple.

"You won't stop worrying until this baby is out of me and sitting on your lap, will you?" she asked, and pulled back to see his face.

Miklo grinned. "How well you know me." Pulling her closer again, he put one arm around her shoulders and the other on her abdomen. He never tired of feeling his child stirring inside her.

Beneath his hand, the muscles of her abdomen tensed, and she gave a surprised gasp.

"What is it?" he asked, near panic as he saw the tension in her face.

"I think you're going to be a father sooner than we thought."

Jeannine took a deep breath and closed her eyes as the pain passed. "Well, maybe not. The pain just went away. Maybe the baby is just moving around."

"That's a relief. You're not due for two weeks yet."

"I know, but babies come when they're ready, not when the calendar says." Jeannine gasped as another pain seared through her abdomen. "Miklo?"

"Yes?"

"I think we need to leave. I don't care what the calendar says, I think we're going to be having a baby today."

Miklo let out a whoop of happiness. "We're having a baby today!" he yelled to this family and friends. With a hand around her shoulders he led her to the door. "Stay here, and I'll bring the car around."

"Hurry," she said as she held on to Seferino. Jolanda hovered nearby.

"Don't worry. This baby is going to be fine." Seferino kissed Jeannine's cheek and held her until Miklo returned. "I'm not so sure he should be driving, though."

"You can tell him that." Jeannine gasped as another pain sliced through her.

"Christo!" Seferino yelled, and motioned for his son to come forward. "You need to drive them to the hospital. Now."

"Really?" Christo's surprised eyes widened. "I get to drive the Jag?"

"Who said you get to drive the Jag?" Miklo asked as he entered the restaurant.

"I do," Seferino said. "Focus on your wife and baby. Christo will get you there in one piece." He patted Miklo on the shoulder. "We'll be there soon."

"Everyone?" Jeannine asked, her eyes wide.

"Of course, everyone. We will welcome your little one into our family."

Jeannine bit her lip and tried not to laugh at the idea of this large, robust family fitting into the waiting room at the hospital without causing a riot.

"Let's go," Miklo said, and assisted her into the car.

Christo hopped into the driver's side of the waiting car. "Let's get this show on the road."

"What if my waters break in the car?" Jeannine asked.

"Drive fast, Christo," Miklo said, and placed his hand on Jeannine's abdomen.

"You got it."

* * *

Ten long hours later, Miklo held his son in his arms. The proud father took the healthy newborn to the nursery window, showed him off to the family and then returned to Jeannine's side.

"You made a beautiful baby boy, wife," Miklo said. He sat in the chair beside Jeannine's bed.

"With you as his father, it was easy," she said, and reached out to hold the baby.

Miklo watched as his son suckled at Jeannine's breast. It was a sight that he had anticipated for two years and now he savored the sight. A bitter-sweet ache stirred in his heart at the past that had died and for the baby that had just begun life.

With Jeannine's love and support, he had learned to love and to live again.

"Are you okay?" she asked, and reached out one hand to him.

"I'm the happiest man on the planet," he said, and took her hand. "Thanks to you."

"We did it. Together."

Coming next month

HOT-SHOT SURGEON, CINDERELLA BRIDE

by Alison Roberts

Dancing with gorgeous surgeon Tony at a ball makes nurse Kelly feel like a princess – but come morning, it's just a memory. Little does she realise that Tony is searching for his Cinderella…

THE PLAYBOY DOCTOR CLAIMS HIS BRIDE

by Janice Lynn

Kasey Carmichael is horrified when she meets her new colleague – rebel doctor Eric is the man she shared one passionate night with! Now Eric must prove he can be trusted with Kasey's heart.

A SUMMER WEDDING AT WILLOWMERE

by Abigail Gordon

GP David Trelawney is wary of relationships, but longs to help nurse Laurel blossom in the warmth of Willowmere. Before summer is out, this handsome doctor will make her his bride!

MIRACLE: TWIN BABIES

by Fiona Lowe

Devastated at the news of her infertility, relationships were *not* on GP Kirby's agenda. Until she meets hot-shot doc Nick Dennison – the attraction is electric! Then a miracle occurs: Kirby is pregnant – with twins!

On sale 7th August 2009

Available at WHSmith, Tesco, ASDA, Eason and all good bookshops.
For full Mills & Boon range including eBooks visit
www.millsandboon.co.uk

Single titles coming next month

A SPECIAL KIND OF FAMILY

by Marion Lennox

When Dr Erin Carmody crashes her car and is rescued by GP Dom Spencer, the intense attraction between them knocks her sideways! As Erin begins to heal, she realises that she belongs with this handsome single father and his boys. But will Dom ever trust that their love is truly real...?

EMERGENCY: WIFE LOST AND FOUND

by Carol Marinelli

Every doctor dreads recognising someone in Casualty, so when James Morrell has to treat his unconscious ex-wife Lorna, he's shocked! As she recovers, James realises he doesn't want Lorna as his patient – he wants her as his wife, this time forever!

On sale 7th August 2009

Available at WHSmith, Tesco, ASDA, Eason and all good bookshops.
For full Mills & Boon range including eBooks visit
www.millsandboon.co.uk

0809/010/MB230

A beautiful collection of classic stories from your favourite Mills & Boon® authors

With Love… Helen Bianchin
Bought Brides
This marriage was going to happen…
Available 17th July 2009

With Love… Lynne Graham
Virgin Brides
A virgin for his pleasure!
Available 21st August 2009

With Love… Lucy Monroe
Royal Brides
Wed at his royal command!
Available 18th September 2009

With Love… Penny Jordan
Passionate Brides
Seduced…
Available 16th October 2009

Collect all four!

www.millsandboon.co.uk